'This is it .... ing
footbɑ .... Mr
Kenni ng after .... t and
enjoy it. Let's hₒₚₑ ₜₒ ₒᵤᵣ day today.

'It will be,' stated Jeff, simply. 'We'll do it. C'mon,
let's get at them!'

With his favourite rallying cry they were off, and
the game was quickly under way with a flurry of
activity in front of both goals. First Tanby had
a   t deflected wide by Andrew, who lunged
aᵤ s to get a foot to a skidding ball.

T   ᵤorner was cleared and Sandford broke
crisₚ y away, Scott finding Dale who switched
it bɑ k to Graham. He made good ground before
relea sing the ball to Alan, and as the blond
striker sidestepped one tackle he hit the ball
o the half-volley. It looked a goal all the way
  til Kevin Baker, their athletic keeper, dived to
his left and clung on to it superbly.

But then Tanby went ahead . . .

ROB CHILDS is a Leicestershire teacher with
m ₙy years experience of coaching and organizing
school and area representative sports teams.
He is the author of a number of previous titles
fₒ ounger readers about football and other
   ₒl sports, including *The Big Match*, *The Big
Hₐ* and *The Big Day*. *Soccer at Sandford* is the
first title in a series about the talented young
footballers at Sandford Primary School.

SOCCER AT SANDFORD

Rob Childs

**ILLUSTRATED BY
TIM MARWOOD**

CORGI YEARLING BOOKS

For all young footballers

SOCCER AT SANDFORD
A CORGI YEARLING BOOK : 0 440 86318 X

First published in Great Britain by Blackie & Sons Ltd

PRINTING HISTORY
Blackie edition published 1980
Corgi Yearling edition published 1993
Reprinted 1993 (twice), 1994, 1995, 1996

Text copyright © 1980 by Rob Childs
Illustrations copyright © 1993 by Tim Marwood
Cover illustration by Tony Kerins

Condition of Sale
This book is sold subject to the condition that it shall not, by way of trade or otherwise, be lent, re-sold, hired out or otherwise circulated without the publisher's prior consent in any form of binding or cover other than that in which it is published and without a similar condition including this condition being imposed on the subsequent purchaser.

This book is set in 12½pt Century Schoolbook by
Phoenix Typesetting, Burley-in-Wharfedale, West Yorkshire.

Corgi Yearling Books are published by Transworld Publishers Ltd,
61–63 Uxbridge Road, Ealing, London W5 5SA,
in Australia by Transworld Publishers (Australia) Pty Ltd,
15–25 Helles Avenue, Moorebank, NSW 2170,
and in New Zealand by Transworld Publishers (NZ) Ltd,
3 William Pickering Drive, Albany, Auckland.

FIFE COUNCIL SCHOOLS SUPPORT	
FC021352	
PETERS	29-Jun-00
JF	£3.99

Contents

CONTENTS

1 Kick-Off

'Hi, Scotty. Back to school again!'

'You don't have to remind me,' Jeff's best friend replied with a grimace. 'What are you so cheerful about anyway? We've got a new teacher today, remember.'

The two boys wandered up the village road towards Sandford Primary School.

'I know, I know,' responded Jeff Thompson, laughing. 'He can't be too bad – he *is* taking us for football as well!'

'Huh, it's all right for you people in Year Six,' muttered Scott who was just as soccer mad. 'It's not fair that us younger ones never get a chance to play in the school team.'

'Well, don't worry, I felt just the same last year. Your turn will come.'

At morning assembly a sea of faces swung round to inspect the newcomer as Mr

Turner, the Headmaster, introduced him to the children. 'We haven't enjoyed much sporting success here for several years,' he boomed on, 'so let's wish Mr Kenning and his teams good luck this season. Try your best, that's the thing, everybody.'

In the classroom afterwards Mr Kenning was kept busy settling himself and the pupils in after the long summer holidays. But when the playtime bell sounded and most of the class trooped cheerfully out of the door Scott, Jeff and two other lads, Ricky Collier and Dale Gregson, grouped themselves around his desk.

Jeff spoke first. 'Do you think we'll have a good team this year, Mr Kenning?'

The teacher laughed. 'Well, I shall have to see you all play before I can answer that question. Did any of you play last year?'

'None of us,' answered Dale. 'We were too young.'

Mr Kenning looked surprised. 'That's a

pity, it would have been good experience for you. Age won't matter from now on anyway, boys, it's ability that counts. Anyone who's good enough will be considered for a team place as far as I'm concerned.'

The lads were delighted to hear that, especially Scott Peters, who suddenly became very enthusiastic about school.

'But everyone will have to keep playing well in order to stay in,' continued the teacher. 'I'm looking forward to seeing how many stars we have here!'

They all grinned. 'We can't wait to start,' said Ricky. 'We've been dreaming about it all through the holidays.'

Mr Kenning immediately became very popular as the other younger boys quickly heard the good news about their unexpected opportunity to play for the school. He put a notice on the sports board for footballers to write their names for practices. Very soon over thirty names

appeared, mostly from his own Class 2 and Mrs Cowper's Class 1, but also some from the lower junior classes.

'Any talent here?' he asked Mr Turner, showing him the list.

'Oh yes, I've seen some of them play during games lessons. But they'll need a lot of encouragement and help. It'll be a real treat for them this year to have someone as keen as you to improve their football. It should make quite a difference.'

'They're certainly raring to go already.'

'Jeff Thompson especially, no doubt,' smiled the Head. 'He ought to have been able to play last year.'

He skimmed through the list again, picking out various names. 'There is one missing, however, which should be on.'

'Oh, who's that?' asked Mr Kenning with interest.

'Gary . . . Gary Clarke. But you'll soon get to hear of him.'

There was a hint of warning in his voice

10

that surprised the new teacher.

A few more names were added to the list on the noticeboard later that day, and right at the bottom in very careless fashion was scrawled simply . . . Gary.

'I'll see what you all can do today,' said Mr Kenning at the first practice. 'Then in future you'll mostly be in smaller groups trying to improve your skills.'

They had been sorted out into their favourite positions for the trial game, with Ricky Collier in goal for the Greens, while a youngster from Year Four had volunteered as keeper for the Whites.

'We've got a much stronger team than the Greens,' chuckled Dale to his pal and fellow striker Graham Ford. 'We'll tear their defence apart!'

'Hope so,' said Graham, his black face breaking up into a wide grin, 'but Ricky's pretty good, you know.'

Jeff ran up alongside. 'Where's Gary? Isn't he playing?'

'Told me he'd forgotten his boots and just went off home,' explained Dale, with a shrug.

The teacher gathered the boys together before the start. 'I want to see you all helping one another during the game. Find space and call for the ball if you're in a good position for a pass.'

The game kicked off with Graham sweeping the ball out to Dale on the left wing. But before he'd properly controlled it, ginger-haired full back Jimmy McDowell came in with great determination to win the ball.

'Well done, Jimmy,' called Mr Kenning. 'That's the way, mark tightly.'

Jeff Thompson immediately impressed in midfield for the Whites, tackling strongly, taking players on and using the ball intelligently. He seemed to have more time than the others to do what he wanted, always a sign of a good footballer.

'He'd make an inspiring captain,' thought the teacher. 'He has authority on the field and seems a popular lad too.'

Scott, Jimmy and Ricky all showed up well in the hard-pressed Green defence. Ricky's performance was especially interesting, as his position was crucial. Mistakes in goal were fatal, and a team needed a confident, reliable keeper. He looked very promising, coming out time and again to narrow an angle or to save a shot, like when he stopped an excellent effort from Graham right on the line with a brilliant reflex dive.

'Well saved, Ricky,' shouted Jeff. 'We just can't beat you today.'

But they did at last, just before the half-time breather, when Dale pulled the ball back square for midfield man John Robinson to steer into the far corner.

After several pieces of advice and

encouragement to both sides the Greens surprisingly equalized with their first attack of the second half. Right winger David Woodward tried a long-range shot which crept just inside a post with young Robin Tainton unable to reach it.

As the game went on, however, the White team's overall strength proved decisive, with further goals coming from Graham and then Jeff.

The teacher suddenly noticed a lone figure appearing round the corner of the school building. He recognized Gary Clarke and went over to him as the match continued. He didn't give much of an excuse, but Mr Kenning sensed something a little deeper behind the boy's apparently flippant attitude, perhaps a note of regret at missing out on the action.

'I expected you here, Gary. I've been told that you can play quite well, but you'll have to show me that for yourself.'

14

The boy looked down at the ground, but Mr Kenning continued, wanting to set their future relationship on firm lines. 'If you don't turn up you are only letting yourself down. And if you're not interested, then certainly neither am I. It's up to you entirely.' He let the message sink in. 'Do you understand, Gary?'

Gary nodded, but gave no indication of what may have been passing through his mind. He brightened up visibly, though, when he was offered the chance to show his skills. Quickly he slipped into a spare green shirt to join in for the last part of the game, to the obvious annoyance of some of the other players.

'Thanks for turning up,' Scott remarked, sarcastically. 'You needn't have bothered.'

'Shut up, Peters, you're not doing any good without me.'

'No arguing, you two. Get on with the game,' cut in Mr Kenning straightaway.

But when Gary received the ball for the first time he tried to be too clever. He jinked past two tackles but then took on one man too many and the chance was wasted.

'Not too much, Gary,' called the teacher. 'It's a team game. Look for possible passes if there's time.'

The level of ability shown by many of the boys in the match had been high. Graham and Dale's partnership up front looked especially sharp as they linked up once more to provide Graham with a second goal near the end.

Mr Kenning delayed the final whistle a minute later when Gary broke away. This time he did play a neat one-two pass with David Woodward, then burst past a weary defender. He looked as though he had taken it too far, but suddenly in a flash of obvious class he screwed the ball back into the goal from a very narrow angle.

'Well, he's an individualist and no mistake,' the teacher reflected, with a sigh. 'Very talented, but we'll have to wait to see whether he fits in with the rest of the team.'

'Nice goal, Gary,' called Jeff through the crowd to the boy trailing behind the cheerful group on their way back to the changing room. The others were all chattering amongst themselves about their performances, leaving the latecomer to bring up the rear on his own.

Mr Kenning heard the remark, and the boy's generous attitude convinced him that Jeff would be an ideal team captain.

He called him over to one side. 'Well played, Jeff. A fine game.'

The lad smiled, pleased with the compliment, but this turned to an expression of great pride and delight when he was offered the captaincy.

'It's an important job, Jeff. You'll have

to take decisions and give instructions to people during a game as you think fit. Players need the right kind of encouragement, and the skipper often needs to set the example by showing them what he wants himself. But I'm sure you can do it.'

'Thanks, Mr Kenning, that's great.' Jeff beamed. 'I'll do my best. We're going to have a fantastic season!'

2 Seven-a-Side

During the impressive practices over the following fortnight, Mr Kenning decided with some difficulty on the two teams that the school would enter in the annual Seven-a-Side tournament.

Amid great interest and excitement he pinned the team sheet on the sports noticeboard for the eager boys to see. He had written them in a basic 3-1-2 formation.

Sandford 'A':

Ricky Collier

Jimmy McDowell   Scott Peters   Paul Curtis

Jeff Thompson (*capt*)

Graham Ford   Dale Gregson

Sub: Ian Freeman

Sandford 'B':

Robin Tainton

Sammy King   Andrew Fisher   Lee Robinson

John Robinson (*capt*)

David Woodward   Gary Clarke

Sub: Dean Walters

The chosen ones were delighted and there was a lot of good-natured joking. Even Gary seemed to smile, though secretly he had wanted to be in the stronger 'A' side. As promised, several younger lads had been included too. Jimmy, Scott and 'B' team substitute Dean Walters were in Year Five, whilst keeper Robin Tainton and defenders Sammy King and John's younger brother, Lee Robinson, were still only in Year Four, their second year of the juniors. This would be a great day for them!

The two sides practised on the Wednesday afternoon before the event. The boys quickly adjusted to the different rules on the small pitch: for instance nobody apart from the goalkeeper was allowed inside the special semi-circle area. As they all got used to their various positions they worked out a few simple tactics, and it soon became obvious that Jeff and John were the vital link-men in each team. They had the important job of helping in defence

and prompting swift attacks.

'Drop back and mark when we lose the ball, but always leave one player up front to clear the ball to,' advised Mr Kenning. 'Then when we attack let's see the full backs breaking down the wings to support the main forwards as long as it's safe to do so.'

'It'll be all action, won't it!' enthused Jeff. 'Up and down the pitch all the time, defending then attacking.'

'That's right,' agreed the teacher. 'It needs good teamwork, helping out in defence and trying to get plenty of shots in yourselves. I'm sure you can get the season off to a good start on Saturday.'

A convoy of parents' cars met on the drizzly morning ready to set off for the tournament in Frisborough, the local town, but the weather failed to dampen the high spirits of the boys.

'Fifteen. Who's missing?' asked Jeff.

'Gary,' answered Scott, not seeming surprised.

The teacher sent the party on ahead while he went to look for Gary at his home nearby.

'He got up late,' said his mother, annoyed, 'and I've sent him out on some errands before he can go off footballing.'

Mr Kenning wasn't going to get involved in a family issue. 'Will he be able to come to Frisborough later?' he asked simply.

'Possibly,' she said, uninterested. 'He's got an old bike. It won't hurt him if he really wants to play. But he'll have to do all his chores first.'

'Well tell him I hope he can make it. He'll have a game if his team's still in.'

While the teacher was driving into town on his own the rest of the boys were proudly pulling on the smart all-red kit of Sandford School for the first time in their lives. They were all a little nervous, but still

optimistic about their chances.

Mr Kenning arrived in time to watch the 'A' team trouncing Parthorpe School 'B' team 5-0 in the first round of the competition. Graham and Dale grabbed two goals each, and the final one in the fifteen-minute game was scored by defender Paul Curtis, a stylish left-footed lad. They could scarcely conceal their delight.

'Put a coat on to keep warm in between matches,' advised their sports-master. 'There are harder games to come.'

Sandford 'B' had a lucky bye into the second round, but here they were drawn against Little Beaton 'A'.

'Right boys, we haven't come here to get knocked out straightaway, have we?' Mr Kenning encouraged them before the start. 'Try your best, and keep going right to the end.'

'Come on, let's give them a shock,'

shouted skipper John Robinson as they ran on to the pitch.

Dean Walters was playing up front in Gary's absence, and he almost scored in the first minute but earned a corner instead. This was still important, however, because if the game were drawn the team with more corners would go through.

Watched by the 'A' team, goalkeeper Robin was the next to win their cheers. He clung on to a long range power-drive which seemed destined for the corner of the net, and the young lad felt a lot better after that.

'Get the ball clear a bit quicker and follow it up,' was the half-time advice. 'Test them out with breakaways.'

Having expected an easy win, Little Beaton became anxious and quarrelsome when they couldn't score, and their play suffered as a result. Even so, Sandford were well behind on corners, but then

from one of these Robin kicked the ball hard upfield quickly. In their desperate search for goals Little Beaton had left gaps at the back, and as Dean jabbed the ball on, David Woodward found himself with a clear run at goal. He remained calm and coolly sidefooted the ball home before he entered the prohibited goal area.

'C'mon, concentrate,' yelled John after they'd all mobbed the scorer. 'It's not over yet.'

But although they conceded two more corners and had to be rescued by a tremendous diving save by Robin, they managed to hang on for a memorable 1-0 victory.

It was the 'A' team's turn again next. They were trailing at the interval, but eventually beat Gateway Village School 2-1. Second-half goals from Jeff and Graham saved them from a surprise exit.

Both teams scored very good wins in the Quarter-Finals. Jimmy McDowell hit a fine first goal for the 'A's in a 3-1 success. He was so overjoyed that he still hadn't settled down properly when the boy whom he was supposed to be marking equalized for Gainsville 'A'.

'That's a good lesson learnt,' thought Mr Kenning, sensing from Jimmy's sorrowful face that the boy had realized his mistake. 'Keep your mind on the game,' he shouted to him. 'Get stuck in again.'

He did too with great determination, and hardly allowed his opponent another kick of the ball. It was Dale who put them safely through to the Semi-Finals with two goals in the second period.

The 'B's did remarkably well to join them there by defeating the only other surviving 'B' team from Fairway School 3-2 on corners. John's early goal had been cancelled out late in the game, when they

relaxed too soon, thinking the game was as good as won.

Luckily the draw kept the Sandford teams apart, and this gave them the unbelievable chance of meeting in the Final itself if somehow they could both win their matches. The teacher had both teams together briefly.

'Don't ease up near the end, whatever the score,' he warned. 'You've all seen what can happen if you do. Remember that football lesson today. Play your hardest to the final whistle of every game. Now good luck, go out and enjoy these games. You're all doing great!'

He didn't tell the 'B's that their opponents, the 'A' team from Tanby School, were the favourites to win the trophy. Tanby had swept the board the previous year, winning the League and the Cup, and looked strong enough again this season to retain the Sevens cup they won last time too!

After only a few minutes Tanby were two goals ahead with neat, clever moves. Responding to touchline encouragement from parents and friends the 'B' team stuck to their task creditably, but their own attacks were petering out against the solid Tanby defence. It would need something special to get back into the game.

And here it was, perhaps! Mr Kenning turned round to see Gary, flushed and weary from his rapid bike ride. Sympathetic now to the boy's home problems, he quickly explained the situation to him. 'Here's your chance, Gary, get ready for the second half.'

Andrew Fisher was struggling manfully to hold his hard-pressed defence together. Sammy and Lee were being outpaced by their speedy attackers, and John and Dean had to spend most of their time trying to help out, leaving David all alone up front. Even the boys were glad to see Gary at the break.

'Well done,' the teacher encouraged. 'You're certainly up against a good team here. We'll see if Gary can give us some goals now in place of Dean.'

But the second half started badly: a corner was deflected in to put them three down. Gary, however, was determined that he should not have cycled all that way for nothing. From the centre he attempted a solo run ignoring everyone else, but finally lost the ball.

'Come on,' shouted David, 'pass it! We won't score any like that.'

Tanby began to coast along now, but this unexpected casualness allowed John to find Gary lurking in space near to goal. Without hesitation the new striker stroked the ball skilfully into the far corner of the net.

Hope was revived and Sandford found new spirit. They surged back into the attack, and Gary at last passed to David who sent a good shot only narrowly wide. Then, in the very last minute, Gary had a run on his own again and this time it came off. He beat two men before curling the ball beautifully out of the goalkeeper's reach.

Only 2-3 down, but that was it. Tanby leapt in the air with relief as the final whistle blew.

The boys were naturally disappointed to have been knocked out, but they soon cheered up with all the praise that was showered upon them for their performance. They turned their attention now to supporting their friends in the other Semi-Final.

The 'A' team wanted to have a crack at Tanby themselves and were in no mood to mess about. Kelworth 'A' were swept aside ruthlessly. Graham and Dale, backed up by Jeff, proved much too lively for their slow-moving defence. After a

succession of corners Jeff stormed through to notch the first, and Graham made it 2-0 by half-time from Jimmy's pass.

But soon afterwards misfortune struck. Scott was accidently kicked on the ankle when tackling, and was in too much pain to carry on. Blond-haired Ian Freeman, who normally liked to play in midfield, jumped at the chance of taking Scott's place at centre-back. But he was never really tested, and two goals by Graham and Dale settled the match with a consolation reply from Kelworth sandwiched in between in the 4-1 scoreline.

The scene was set for a dramatic Final clash between the 'A' sides of Sandford and Tanby schools! The 'Reds' versus the 'Sky-Blues' . . .

The sun had broken through and was glinting on the trophy and medals waiting on the table for presentation. Both teams had taken a short rest and were now raring to go for their ten-minutes-each-way Final match.

Only Scott felt miserable, his ankle too sore to play. The others needed little urging now from the teacher; it was up to them, and they knew what they had to try to do.

Tanby started exactly as before, attempting to sew the match up in the first few minutes. They were thwarted first by a good save from Ricky, and then by Paul's last-ditch tackle which conceded a corner. Jimmy cleared this up to Graham, who tried a speculative shot on the turn which sailed high over the bar.

'Steady,' yelled Jeff. 'You had time to get balanced properly first.'

Tanby's early pressure, however, did earn them the first goal, their main striker giving Ricky no chance from close-in. But the 'A's had a bit more ability than their pals in the 'B' team, and didn't fall into the same trap of being pressed

back too much in their own half.

If they weren't allowed to play the ball out with short passes, then they hit long ones into spaces for Graham and Dale to run on to. This kept the Tanby defence on their toes, and prevented them pushing too many players forward.

It was on one of these breaks that Dale was set free down the left flank, his favourite position. He had time to pinpoint Graham moving in, and his friend met the centre perfectly with the side of his boot just outside the area to level it at 1-1.

The match really came to life now, and there was loud cheering from the touchlines for both teams.

The equalizing goal put Sandford on top for a while, and they took a well deserved lead just before the interval when a rapid series of interpassing ended with skipper Jeff firmly striking the ball home, and leaping high with delight.

At half-time they were very confident. 'We've got them,' gasped Dale, 'I think we can do it now.'

'Course we can,' agreed Jimmy, with relish. 'We held them at the start, and now we're in front.'

'We've still another ten minutes to play, remember,' stressed Jeff, taking his captain's job seriously. 'Don't let up – they're still dangerous.'

But despite his words of warning the second period began disastrously when Ian, the replacement defender, went into the keeper's area under pressure to intercept a pass. The free kick was cleverly rolled back, and the ball was hammered past an unsighted Ricky Collier to make it all square once more.

Tanby had their tails up now, and Ian quickly had to make up for his error with an excellent, decisive tackle. But somehow in the next swift attack the ball was

touched through the smallest of gaps and rolled agonizingly into the corner of the goal.

Sandford were now 2-3 down on goals and also 0-2 on corners. Mr Kenning was beginning to wish the rules allowed him to bring Gary on again after his earlier display. There he was, standing near his bicycle, still wearing his football boots. He looked as disappointed as the rest of them.

But they all reckoned without the determination and fighting spirit of Jeff Thompson! As they trooped back for the restart, he went round all the players urging them to keep their heads up. 'There's still time,' he was heard to say to Dale. 'Come on, let's get back at them.'

This was a real test of character, and the boys responded magnificently. Tanby on the other hand became a little over-confident, and they were made to pay in full. Sandford piled on the pressure, winning one corner back, and then at last another when Graham's shot was turned round a post.

'Corners level. Now for a goal!' shouted Jeff.

His corner was cleared, but only as far as Jimmy. He weaved past one opponent and then let fly. The ball thwacked against the near post, beating the goalkeeper, rebounded over to hit the other, and then flipped over the line before he could recover.

A tremendous cheer went up, and even Mr Kenning threw his arms into the air with excitement.

After the jubilations the team buckled down straightaway to keep their defence tight after their previous experience, and at the final whistle the two sides were dead level!

So the Final itself would have to be decided on penalties, three players from each side to take them in turn. In the middle of all the noise and excitement the penalty-takers tried to keep as calm as possible. Dale, Graham and Jeff prepared themselves, and Dale opened the scoring confidently by tucking the ball past their keeper, Kevin Baker. Tanby's first player did likewise, giving Ricky no time even to move. One each.

A weary Graham, having run himself almost to a standstill in the matches, hit the next penalty cleanly but without much power. He sank to the ground in despair as Baker chose the right way to dive and stopped it on the line.

Tanby's next kicker took a long run and smacked the ball fiercely. Ricky dived blindly, but the wrong way. He didn't even see the ball sail wide of the other post into the scattering spectators. Still

1-1 as the tension mounted.

It was left to the two captains, Jeff Thompson and Simon Walsh.

Jeff steadied himself, decided to side-foot it and hoped. Again Baker guessed correctly and got a hand to it, but this time it wasn't enough and he only succeeded in turning the ball up into the roof of the net. 2-1 to Sandford.

If Simon Walsh scored too, other players would have a try until somebody missed. The pressure was really on him – and on Ricky as well.

A relieved Jeff slapped Ricky on the back and joked to him as he took up his position. Ricky grinned, and it helped him to feel more relaxed. Again he decided to dive to his left as Walsh hit it low and hard, but Ricky's gamble this time was correct. He got both hands behind the ball and somehow clung on to it!

The Sandford supporters immediately

shouted and danced in delight, and all the players ran to lift Ricky off his feet like a hero. The dispirited Tanby side slumped down in anticlimax, after being so near to winning themselves.

A very proud Jeff received the Sevens trophy for the school, and then watched as each boy in both teams received their individual awards. The losers were cheering up quickly as they received special applause in consolation and encouragement for their fine display.

'What a fantastic start to the season!' Jeff cried as parents tried to get the team lined up for family photographs. 'What an incredible day!'

A photograph of the triumphant boys, all big smiles and muddied shirts, holding up their trophies for the pressman's camera, appeared in the local newspaper, and this was pinned on the noticeboard. The report was added underneath and they all read it over and over again, enjoying the novelty of seeing their names in print, and joking about the picture.

It wasn't going to be the last time they were featured on the sports pages of the *Frisborough Journal*. They would see to that!

3 League Ups and Downs

'The League matches start at home this Saturday against Fairway School,' read Scott Peters glumly from the noticeboard.

'Won't you be able to play?' asked Jimmy McDowell.

'No chance. Mum says I've got to rest my ankle for a while yet. Can't even do P.E. or anything.' He tried to brighten up. 'I'll be here to watch, though, don't worry!'

After the week's practices Mr Kenning pinned up the team sheet, setting it out in a basic 4-3-3 formation, but the boys already knew they had plenty of freedom to move into different positions as they thought fit during a game.

Team:

Ricky Collier

Jimmy McDowell Ian Freeman Andrew Fisher Paul Curtis
John Robinson   Jeff Thompson (*capt*)   Dean Walters
David Woodward   Graham Ford   Dale Gregson
Subs: Gary Clarke, Sammy King

He had named Gary as substitute again somewhat reluctantly after his Sevens display, but the boy had had another of his regular periods of being off school without a proper excuse and so had missed the team practices. According to his teacher Mrs Cowper, all this time away made him

43

fall behind with his work and he tended to be lazy in class anyway. Dean Walters deserved the place more than the unpredictable Gary at the moment.

The day came at last and after their success in the Sevens tournament Sandford began very confidently in their freshly laundered all-red strip in front of quite a gathering of keen parents and friends. They remembered the school finishing second to bottom of the twelve teams in the League last season, eleven games altogether, playing each other once only, and they were determined to prove that Sandford would be no pushovers again this year.

The match began at a fast and furious pace with both goalkeepers in busy action, Ricky being fortunate when Paul kicked a shot off the line.

Fairway, however, were beginning to put their game together very impressively, and Jeff and John were having to spend more and more time helping out in defence. Almost inevitably, just before the 25-minute first half was complete, the visitors went ahead when a long through ball to the centre-forward caught Sandford on the wrong foot.

The defenders thought he was offside and half-stopped but Mr Kenning, the referee, determined to be fair, decided not. Ricky came out bravely and managed to block the ball but it rolled free for the attacker to poke it into the unguarded net.

'Our forwards have hardly seen the ball for the last ten minutes,' the teacher remarked at half-time. 'You've got to get back into this game. Often the best form of defence is attack – give them something to worry about.'

'That goal was offside!' protested Ian in annoyance.

'No it wasn't,' Mr Kenning said firmly. 'I don't want to hear any complaints of referees' decisions at all this season from anybody. Understand? Play to the whistle. Don't stop and wait for it in case you're wrong yourself. Just concentrate on your own game. It's important to remember that.'

The second half began better with David and Graham shooting for goal, but Dale was making little progress against his full back.

'Come on, Dale,' encouraged Jeff. 'Pass it quickly, you can't dribble it past him.'

But again it was Fairway who made the most of their chances, going 2-0 ahead as the home defence got into a tangle from a corner.

Some boys would have let their heads go down at this point if it hadn't been for Jeff's intervention. He hated the thought of losing their first League game. 'Right, enough of that!' he called across to the dispirited figures. 'There's plenty of time left yet. We can still win, we've got to try harder.'

He finished with his favourite saying, 'Let's get at 'em!'

The Fairway boys were still celebrating and not expecting Jeff's dynamism. He got the ball from the restart, carried it forward, exchanged quick passes with David on the right wing to go past a couple of defenders, and then let fly with a tremendous right foot shot from well outside the penalty area.

The keeper could only stand and gawp as the speeding missile flew over his head and thumped against the top of the crossbar before rebounding out of play.

This inspiration was exactly the boost needed, and the team immediately responded to such positive leadership. Twice more Fairway were forced to scramble the

ball away, and then Sandford at last broke through.

Dean, backing up a run by Dale, hit the loose ball after the full back's successful tackle straight across into the middle. Jeff lunged in but only snicked it and spun it into Graham's path. There was no doubting the black striker's leap of sheer delight after he'd rammed the ball up into the roof of the net.

But ten minutes later it remained 2-1 to Fairway despite a lot of exciting attacking from both sides. Twice Ricky had moved smartly to save, and Andrew Fisher had once saved the day with a crucial, well-timed tackle near the penalty spot.

It was time for Gary to show his paces.

Jeff led the applause for a disappointed Dale as the winger trailed off, but this special attention quickly cheered him up! Gary, however, was a let-down. He looked frail and unconcerned, and the strong full back had no trouble dealing with him either. Mr Kenning was as baffled as anybody. Gary lost the ball easily, refused to pass, and only once managed any kind of a shot – and this trickled into the keeper's hands.

Time was running out as the rest of the team struggled on. Whatever the others were thinking, Jeff was driven by only one thought – they must get the equalizer! But even he almost left it too late. Inside the final minute on Mr Kenning's watch Jeff hit a long ball out to David who found himself in space for the first time, his marker having flagged. David sped past him, kept the ball in play, steadied himself and looked up.

Almost everyone seemed to have crowded into the area for the cross, so instead he surprised them all by screwing the ball back low for John Robinson, steaming up inside him in support.

John belted it in his stride, falling over as he did so. He'd made contact cleanly enough, though, and somehow kept it down, and the poor keeper just couldn't get a clear sight of it through the ruck of players in front of him.

He saw it late and dived to his left but wasn't able to reach it. There was the ball spinning and nestling in the net behind him. Two goals each, and no time left for either side to alter the scoreline.

As the two teams gave the traditional three cheers for each other, Fairway's teacher congratulated Mr Kenning on Sandford's spirited come-back. 'You'll take some stopping this season, I can see that,' he smiled. 'You must be very pleased with them.'

He was indeed, and remained optimistic that they would enjoy a successful year. But there were still a few matters that would need time, patience and under-

50

standing to sort out. And one of these problems was undoubtedly Gary Clarke!

Scott had recovered enough to play in the next two games, replacing Ian, who had performed very well in his unfamiliar position. Scott's better defensive qualities, however, were not much required in easy wins. They defeated the small village school of Parthorpe 6-0 with the help of a hat-trick from Graham, and goals from the three 'D's: David, Dale and Dean.

Ullesby School were the next victims. Paul Curtis opened the scoring in a 5-1 triumph, after a fine run up the left wing. Jeff added the second, David scored two more, and Graham grabbed the fifth. Nine-year-old Sammy King had a great thrill in this game, coming on for Andrew to gain useful experience in the school team.

Gary remained unsettled. He attended the practices, but Mrs Cowper threatened

to stop his football if he didn't buck up
his work efforts in class. Mr Kenning was
pleased to hear later that Gary's stand-
ard did improve, as it showed how much
football meant to him. He was sure that
the team would need Gary's extra skill
and flair sooner or later against tighter
defences. They might welcome that spark
of individuality and selfishness on the pitch
one day, to give them a crucial goal out of
the blue.

That occasion came sooner than even
the teacher anticipated, and Gary was not
there to help.

The boys had gathered at the usual meeting place for the short trip into Frisborough
to play Fullerton School in confident, relaxed mood. When substitute Gary failed to
appear at all nobody seemed too bothered.

'It doesn't matter,' said Scott. 'We don't
need him. I bet he's sulking because he
can't get into the team.'

'It's always the same,' complained Graham. 'I'm fed up with him being late.'

Mr Kenning understood the boy's unpopularity to some extent, but he knew too that it wasn't always Gary's fault. Something must have happened at home to prevent him from coming.

They left without him, and went 1-0 up soon after the start. Dale weaved past two defenders and lashed the ball home with great glee. John Robinson added another from David's pass, and even when Fullerton replied just before half-time their 2-1 lead looked secure. The boys sensed little danger.

'We'll take them apart in the second half,' said David.

'Another easy win,' remarked substitute Ian, rather disappointed that he wouldn't be needed.

'Maybe,' replied Jeff as they finished

their oranges, 'but we'll have to watch their two big attackers, or they might give us some trouble.'

'No chance,' answered Scott. 'We've got this game in our pockets.'

Mr Kenning repeated Jeff's little warning about over-confidence, but he too expected them to carry their advantage through to the end.

The team, however, soon saw the wisdom of his words. They were hauled level straightaway, when a strong attack finished with Ricky ruefully picking the ball out of the net. But still they refused to believe in Fullerton's revival, and continued to stroke the ball about leisurely, expecting to score again each time they attacked.

Even when Ricky made a desperate lunge to fingertip a shot around the post the mounting danger was ignored. Despite warning shouts from the touchline, one of the tall lads was left completely unmarked from the corner and he jumped up to head the ball powerfully home.

Only now that they had actually fallen behind did they suddenly look worried. They tried to build their attacks more deliberately, but the rhythm had gone and nothing would go right. When Graham shot, an awkward bounce sent his effort way over the bar; a shot from the tireless Jeff was blocked on the line by a defender's knee and Dale hit a post. Increasingly they kept running into trouble; losing the ball, putting passes astray and gradually being pushed back on to the defensive. Ian replaced Dean to add extra power in midfield, but to no avail – they were no longer in control.

Ricky made a couple of fine saves but was eventually beaten for the fourth time by a well struck shot from the right wing.

The defence, now well organized by Scott,

was good enough to prevent any further scoring, but there was no-one up front they could clear the ball to who would be able to run at Fullerton's defence, take them on and cause some problems – someone like Gary, when he put his mind to the job. Mr Kenning felt the boys might begin to appreciate Gary's extra talent after this experience and their 4-2 defeat.

He spoke to them in the quiet changing room. 'If you learn something from such a defeat, then you can turn it into a future victory. Think of what went wrong so that you can try to put it right and not do it again.'

'It won't happen again,' promised Jeff on behalf of the team, who nodded their heads in agreement. 'I mean, we may lose again, but never like that. We just threw it away.'

'We've got to try our hardest all the time, even when we're well on top,' added John.

There was a pause until Andrew Fisher spoke out. 'Wait till we see Gary Clarke, he's really let us down.'

'No,' said Mr·Kenning decisively. 'He's let himself down more, or he may even be ill. He can't be blamed for today's performance.' The teacher looked around at their faces, and decided it was about time that they looked upon Gary in a different, better light. For the boy's own benefit, and for the team's as a whole.

'I'll see him first and get his explanation,' he continued, and then stressed his point. 'You've got to try to encourage Gary, be more friendly towards him, rather than

gang up against him. He's a good player
and an important member of the football
squad. OK?'

The general nods of understanding satisfied him that the boys had all grown up a
little bit today. It would do them no harm to
lose a match, and might even do them some
good. They had to learn to accept a defeat
in the right spirit, just like their victories.
The really important thing was that they
should enjoy their football whatever the
final result, and this they most certainly
did.

As far as the League was concerned, however, Sandford had now taken five points
out of a possible eight. Tanby, he already
knew, had won all four of their opening
games!

4 Up for the Cup

After hearing the result, Gary nearly didn't come to school at all on the Monday. In a funny way he was half pleased about the defeat as it might give him a chance of getting into the team. On the other hand he was expecting serious trouble because of it, possibly even playground fights over his non-appearance.

In the end he arrived late, and it wasn't until morning break that Mr Kenning received his excuses in a quiet corner of his room. He heard the boy out before replying.

'Well I don't know who's to blame, Gary, but if your mother thinks you did something wrong and decided to keep you at home on Saturday morning as punishment, then that's entirely up to her.'

Gary nodded, head down, waiting sadly for any further punishments. He hated

the thought of possibly being banned from playing football – he so much wanted to show everybody that he could be good at something. 'I . . . I didn't mean to . . .' he began before his voice trailed away.

The teacher appreciated his problems at home, but he had no right to interfere there. However he could help Gary at school by encouragement and by building up his self-confidence with personal success on the football field. That is, of course, if the boy allowed him the opportunity. 'I know, Gary, but we must feel that you can be relied upon. What's the point of you playing well enough to make the team, then getting into some silly trouble and having to miss the matches? Your behaviour needs to improve if you want to be considered as part of the squad. It's only fair on the others.'

'I do!' Gary protested.

'Good. I'm glad to hear it. So it's up to you, isn't it?'

Before he sent him outside to play, he finished off. 'We've a Cup match on Saturday, away against Kelworth in the first round of the Frisborough Trophy. Let's see if you can make the team for that, shall we?'

The midweek practices looked promising. They were all trying very hard to make up for their last game and seemed very sharp, none more so than Gary.

Even Scott, usually his fiercest critic, was heard to say a couple of encouraging remarks to him. 'That's more like it, Gary,' he shouted once, after Gary had zipped past one of Jimmy's tigerish tackles and slipped the ball past Robin Tainton for his second goal of the session.

Mr Kenning wanted to give Gary a full game if possible, as a keen and determined Gary would certainly be a real asset to the team. The problem would be who to leave out to make way for him!

Using him as substitute was in many

ways rather a waste of his potential skills. Coming on late he might possibly win you a game in a flash of inspiration, but more often than not there wouldn't be enough time to settle down and adjust to the pace of the match. It was better to give players like Gary more time, to appreciate their full value.

Team selection difficulties were unexpectedly solved, however, when poor Graham Ford, the leading scorer, fell ill on the Thursday. Despite his protests, his mother wrote to say that he was unfit to play.

Graham's loss was a blow to the boys, but the teacher took the opportunity to slot Gary in at centre-forward, and kept his fingers crossed. If Gary didn't click the team could be in serious trouble without Graham's power up front.

In spite of himself Mr Kenning felt a surge of relief when he saw Gary with the party of boys waiting together on Saturday morning. No mistakes at home this time!

Both teams remembered Sandford's 4-1 victory in the Sevens semi-final, and Kelworth threw everything into attack right from the start. They nearly took an important early lead when their tall fair-haired striker Alan Clayton met a cross beautifully with his head, quite a rare thing in primary school football. Ricky knew nothing about it as the ball smashed off his shoulder and looped over the bar for a corner.

'Good lad, Alan, that's showed 'em,' shouted one of the home fans.

Ian put Dale through for a good shot soon after, but the first half mostly belonged to Kelworth. It was just as well that Ricky, Scott and Andrew were on top form. With the midfield players mostly occupied in defence, the Sandford attack saw little of the ball. Gary too had been quiet and subdued because of this, but just before

the interval he received the ball in a bit of space.

He carried it a few metres, and as a defender closed in David screamed for a pass which would have put him clear. Instead, Gary saw his own chance. He skilfully evaded this tackler, slipped another and, still ignoring David, took on the final defender. It was one too many.

Crunch! The big centre-back was taking no chances. He committed a quite blatant nasty foul which dumped Gary firmly and heavily on the ground.

Unused to seeing such bad fouls in school games many of the parents on the touchline were very angry about it. 'His teacher ought to take him off for that – it was disgraceful!' fumed Mr. Thompson, Jeff's father.

'He's been watching too much professional football on television,' Scott's father tried to joke to pass it off.

The free kick came to nothing, and the half-time scoreline remained blank. The boys also were annoyed, not only about the foul, but with Gary as well for holding on to the ball for too long in the first place. Gary was sitting at the side of the group, too busy examining his leg to bother about their complaints.

Mr Kenning calmed them down and made them think about the second half. 'You can win this now, boys. You've taken all they've got. Go out and show them how football should be played properly.'

He also had a quiet word with Gary, now back on his feet. 'Sometimes it's better to go on your own, sometimes others may be in a better position. You have to decide quickly, then either go yourself or pass. Just keep the two alternatives in mind, OK?'

They trooped back on to the field with Jeff's hand on Gary's shoulder in

encouragement. 'Let's have a goal from you, Gary, we need it. But remember, you're not on your own. Be part of the team.'

They grinned at each other, and Gary was pleased that Jeff was being friendly still. He wanted to do well to keep his place as he liked the new prestige in school that being one of the footballers gave him amongst the other boys.

An early chance came to him as the ball ran loose in the penalty area. But instead of shooting as he would normally have done, he checked, hesitated and then pushed the ball back to John who certainly wasn't expecting it from Gary. It gave the defenders time to recover and block John's hurried shot.

'Oh no!' groaned Jeff. 'Now he's passed when he shouldn't have done!'

On the short pitch both keepers were being kept busy as the game swung from end to end. Jeff, now finding more time to come forward, decided to try a long-range shot and smacked a great effort with tremendous force against the crossbar from only just over the halfway line!

Something was bound to give, and it suddenly did so with two goals in three minutes. Jimmy, John, David and finally Gary linked up well, and this time he did pass it just at the right moment inside the full back. David, running cleverly on to it, showed how to keep cool and dribble round a goalkeeper before stroking the ball into the gaping net.

But then Sandford could do nothing to prevent the home side equalizing almost immediately.

Alan Clayton did the damage. He guided a goal kick out to the right wing with his head, took a quick return pass, bustled through Andrew's normally solid challenge, and as Ricky came out to meet him he lofted the ball expertly over his

head and watched it dip just under the bar.

Sandford survived just one more scare when a deflection off Scott luckily landed safely in the arms of the surprised and grateful Ricky, who grinned at his relieved defender. Then Kelworth seemed to fade after their strenuous first-half efforts and the visitors took charge for the last ten minutes.

First David sidefooted the ball against a post, and then it was Gary who stole the show. Ian gave him the ball just inside Kelworth's half. He rode one half-hearted tackle, looked up, and found that this time he really was on his own with the others trailing behind him. He went for goal in great style.

He was ready for the Chopper this time! As he again lunged clumsily in, Gary suddenly and remarkably stopped by dragging the ball back with the sole of his boot. The big defender kicked wildly at thin air and collapsed in an untidy heap.

Gary wheeled quickly round him, flew past a final tackle and before the keeper could begin to narrow the angle, he lashed the ball towards goal. It was struck cleanly and powerfully and the boy did well even to touch it on its way to bulging the net.

Hero Gary was mobbed by his overjoyed teammates and almost carried back to the halfway line. Kelworth were finished and offered little resistance as Dale added a comfortable goal a minute from time from Paul's long clearance to clinch a 3-1 victory to see them into the second round.

Leaving his own boys happily changing, Mr Kenning popped his head into Kelworth's changing area to praise them for their fine display. He recognized the mop of fair hair near the door as belonging to Alan Clayton, and congratulated him especially on his splendid heading.

'Where were you in the Sevens?' he asked.

'We were on holiday still,' the boy replied quietly. 'I was sorry to miss it.'

'Lucky for us you did, I think! Anyway, good luck for the rest of the season.'

As he came out he was stopped by one of their parents. 'I'm Mr Clayton, I'm glad you liked Alan's performance today. You may even be seeing more of him.'

'Oh yes, of course, we're playing you again in a League match after Christmas, aren't we?'

'Well, I didn't mean that. In fact we hope to be moving house soon to a village called Sandford, and I hear the school team there are quite useful!' he grinned in reply.

Mr Kenning couldn't conceal his pleasure at the news. 'Well I certainly hope you do. It'd be marvellous to have Alan joining us!'

What a prospect! The competition for team places would really be keen then. He almost licked his lips in anticipation at the thought of it!

5 Mudlarks

Graham was very quiet in class on his return.

'Cheer up!' encouraged Jeff. 'Gary was good, but we can't do without your goals. We still need you, don't worry.'

'I wonder if I'll be picked for this Saturday, though. You had a great Cup win without me.'

Mr Kenning was in the happy position of having a full squad of sixteen players to choose from for the home League game against The Park junior school from Frisborough. But after a lot of careful consideration he left the team unchanged, naming Graham only as substitute. He intended to bring him on, however, as they would probably need his extra weight and power against a team with an unfortunately rugged reputation.

The Park did play it very hard indeed, and Mr Kenning had to referee firmly to cut out the shoving and elbowing that some of them tried to get away with. He stopped any foul play immediately, and spoke sharply to one boy who went in late and unnecessarily roughly against keeper Ricky. His arm was hurt in the heavy collision, but as it was near the end Ricky carried on. He certainly hadn't had a very eventful morning otherwise, even though The Park's niggling tactics had restricted Sandford to a 2-0 win.

The first-half goal had been a gem. Dale had dropped deep to receive Scott's well aimed clearance, controlled it instantly and pushed a nice pass inside to Ian. Moving forward, he held it until Gary had wriggled free of his marker and then lofted the ball to him.

Going towards goal at speed Gary became aware that soon he was going to

be tackled from behind, so he suddenly swung the ball into the middle with his left foot, an unselfish act he would never have attempted a month before. David met the centre perfectly, steering it first time with the side of his boot into the corner of the net to round off an excellent move.

The competitive match was fought out mostly in The Park's half, and Graham joined in later to replace John to act as a twin spearhead with Gary. Graham it was who earned Sandford's penalty when he was deliberately tripped in the area just as he was about to shoot.

Penalties were rare, and Jeff saw it as one of the captain's responsibilities, although it didn't prove as easy as he had imagined. Their keeper guessed correctly to block his first effort, but with great relief Jeff recovered quickly to smash the rebound back into the billowing net.

With all the chances they had created they were a little disappointed not to have scored more goals, but it was just one of those games where luck wasn't with them.

'Never mind,' said Mr Kenning, 'you kept the pressure on them and showed them how football should really be played. That's the main thing, keep cool and concentrate on your own game, no matter what the opposition are doing.'

The League title race was becoming very interesting. Tanby were still top with maximum points, with Fairway second, closely followed by Sandford themselves.

Winter was also setting in, and many days were cold, wet and windy. Even practices were now held during lunchtime as it was too dark to play after school.

But everyday schoolwork carried on as normal. The Year Six pupils especially had a lot to get through in preparation for their transfer to the secondary school, Frisborough Comprehensive, at the end of the school year. For the footballers, though, enjoyment on the football field rubbed off into the classroom and even made lessons more bearable!

After several days of heavy rain their next match, in Frisborough itself against St John's School, looked in danger of being cancelled. But to the boys' relief, the weather brightened just in time.

'The pitch'll be tricky for sure,' forecast Scott on Thursday. 'I just hope Ricky will be OK to play, though.'

'His arm is still a bit stiff and sore,' replied Jeff, with a worried frown.

'Gary's back again anyway,' chipped in Andrew Fisher.

'Yes, he's really keen now, isn't he?' grinned Scott. 'I used to think he was a bit weird, but he's not so bad once you get to know him better.'

Jeff laughed this time. 'He's certainly changed this year. He's a much better player and nowhere near so greedy with the ball.'

Mr Kenning appeared just then with the team sheet. 'Same again, lads, only I've named Robin Tainton as sub along with Graham in case Ricky's arm gives him any trouble. Robin's coming along well, and is quite reliable.'

They rushed off to break the news to the rather shy Robin who felt completely over-whelmed by all this sudden attention. He began to feel nervous at the mere thought of the match, but he was also very excited at being included in the thirteen.

Although Saturday dawned windy and drizzly, there was still a large party of parents eager to provide transport for the boys and cheer them on. And just when they realized that Gary was missing he tore round the corner into view, arriving with breathless apologies that errands had made him late. Thankfully then they all set off for their last League game before Christmas.

At ten o'clock they kicked off in a clean, red strip. By five minutes past ten most of the shirts, shorts and socks, not to mention boots, legs, hands and even a few faces were smeared, smattered and smothered in dirt, water and mud!

The wind was swirling the rain about and the pitch was a dreadful sight. There were several puddles in the goalmouths and centre circle, and squelchy mud almost everywhere else. Mr Kenning wished he had known about St John's sloping field before. If he'd realized how bad it was he would never have agreed to play.

'Oh well, never mind, it's good experience for them,' said Jeff's father, half-joking. 'They'll have to get used to playing in all kinds of conditions!'

St John's had the slope and the wind in their favour and so hoped to build up a good lead before half-time.

'C'mon, team, we must hold them this half,' urged Jeff.

'Hope we can,' replied John as the home team piled on the early pressure. 'We'll be kicking downhill in the second half and they might be tired by then.'

'I'm tired already!' grinned a filthy Scott, but they knew he was only kidding. Scott revelled in this kind of situation.

'Get the ball clear straightaway, everybody,' shouted Jeff. 'No fancy stuff near our own goal in this mud, it's too dangerous to mess about there.'

Ricky then had to dive across his goal-line to save a long shot. He landed in a pool of dirty water, something he would normally have loved, but Mr Kenning noticed him wince after he had kicked the ball away upfield.

'All right, Ricky?'

The keeper nodded, but continued to rub his bruised arm. The teacher looked at Robin Tainton, huddled under a coat, and wondered what he should do. This pitch was no place for a young goalkeeper to make his school-team début!

Sandford managed the occasional raid themselves, and once Dale glanced a header just wide of the post, but mostly the mud and the slope defeated much forward progress. Often only Gary remained upfield to chase the wild clearances in vain.

Paul kicked one effort off the line, Ian was slightly winded blocking another shot, and after the woodwork had twice saved them they eventually cracked. A low cross skidded through a ruck of bodies and past an unsighted Ricky.

The treacherous surface also hindered St John's attacks, and several times it was only the slippery, greasy ball that prevented them from scoring. Even just keeping their feet in places was difficult enough, and skilful football was virtually out of the question.

Not long before the interval, however, a long kick downfield evaded several legs and the centre-forward found himself in

the clear. Andrew chased him and Ricky raced off his line towards him. All three boys met together at the same spot in a heavy accidental collision.

The ball slithered on towards the empty goal, the mud clawing at it and slowing it down as Jimmy thundered in to try and clear the danger. He dived in and booted it away, but when questioned by the referee he admitted honestly that it was a goal, the ball having trickled over the line just before he reached it.

Mr Kenning was very pleased with Jimmy's sporting attitude, and would have been very cross with him later if he had tried to cover up and get away with it.

Suddenly, in the midst of all the drama they realized that Ricky was still lying on the ground. The teacher ran quickly from the touchline to him to find he'd had another bang on the same arm, and was trying hard to hold back tears of pain.

He immediately led him off and signalled Robin on in his place.

'Good luck, Robin,' Ricky managed to say as they passed, before being hustled off home by his father.

The tense, white-faced goalkeeper was tested straightaway with an awkward shot which skidded along the ground. Robin went down for the ball, but was still stiff from the cold and he missed it. The ball zipped past the outside of the post, and Sandford breathed a sigh of relief.

'Don't worry,' said Jeff, helping him to his feet. 'Keep your eye on it, and try to get your body behind the ball.' The captain grinned and slapped him on the back in encouragement.

The team tried to protect their new keeper as much as they could, covering and blocking even more than before, but they couldn't prevent a close-in effort from a corner which Robin somehow managed

to stop with his legs before Scott scooped it away.

'Well saved, and well done, all of you,' praised their teacher as they gathered round for a very welcome break. 'Get your breath back, and then you can go out and show them how to use their pitch in this weather. Keep the ball near the ground,' he advised, 'or the wind will catch it and blow it out of your reach. Now, what about you wingers?'

'Well, if we stay near the touchlines, it's not quite so muddy, just wet,' observed Dale.

'If they gave us the ball more, we could perhaps make better use of it,' suggested David.

'Good, that's it,' continued Mr Kenning, pleased to see they'd been thinking about the game. 'Stay out wide. That's been their mistake, overcrowding in the muddy middle. Right, use the spaces, and try to get in lots of shots from all angles.'

To Graham's delight, he was called in to replace Ian just behind the main attack, to pick up any half clearances. They trooped back on, bedraggled but full of new spirit despite being two goals down.

'Now it's our turn!' David goaded one of the opponents.

St John's, packing back their whole team, held out for five minutes and then the floodgates opened. David started it from the right wing, slithering past his full back and hitting a hard, low centre right into the goalmouth. In the confusion of legs stretching for it, the ball cannoned off a defender's knee and flew past his own stranded keeper.

St John's managed to break away from the restart and put in a shot, but Robin was alert and safely clutched the ball to his chest, which did his own confidence, and that of the team, a world of good. He kicked it well downfield with the help of the strong

wind, Graham headed it on while Gary dummied inside, leaving Dale with space to advance. His shot curled away against the far post but John Robinson, following up, tucked the rebound into the net.

Two goals each and Sandford were on the rampage!

They proved too strong for the crumbling home side, now jaded and buckling under the onslaught. The ground was too heavy for Gary's more delicate skills but he worked hard for the team by distracting the defence with good decoy runs, which the boys had never really appreciated until now.

Stronger, more forceful players like Graham and Jeff came into their own, ploughing through the sticky conditions and causing havoc. Graham belted home the third, laid on another for David weaving in from the wing, and then exchanged passes with Jeff, while a defender was bogged down in the mud and unable to turn, for the captain to steer in the fifth.

Despite a bombardment of further shots from almost everybody the plucky goalkeeper, with help from the posts and crossbar, prevented any more goals. A 5-2 result, and both teams, wet through and muddy, thoroughly deserved their hot drink back in the school building afterwards. They joked about the filthy state they were in, all trying to brag that they had more mud on them than anybody else!

As they noisily celebrated their victory Mr Kenning quietly reflected that it was the second round of the Cup next week, away at Fullerton – the scene of their only defeat so far. Ricky was unlikely to be fit in time, and though he had been pleased with Robin's performance, he couldn't help wondering whether the boy was ready yet for such a vital, testing game.

Special goalkeeping practice during the week, he decided with a rueful smile – everything might depend on how well young Robin played!

6 Cup Cliffhanger

News arrived in school that Tanby, like themselves, had drawn with Fairway, dropping a point at last. It left the top four positions in the Christmas League table very close together as the boys could see from the noticeboard.

	P	W	D	L	F	A	PTS
Tanby	6	5	1	0	31	8	11
Sandford	6	4	1	1	22	9	9
Fairway	6	3	3	0	19	7	9
Fullerton	6	4	1	1	20	10	9

Five games still to play and the title was wide open, especially as Sandford and Fullerton both had yet to play Tanby.

'Phew, it's tight at the top!' breathed Jeff.

'Goal difference might be important at

the end so we'd better try and score as many as we can in every game,' David pointed out.

'And,' interrupted Scott, adding a defender's viewpoint, 'make sure we don't let too many in ourselves at the same time.'

'Scotty's right,' agreed Jeff. 'We've got to look for extra goals without getting careless and leaving big gaps in our own defence.'

'I'm not very good at maths,' joked Jimmy. 'Why don't we save ourselves all the bother of working out goal difference by winning the League by ten clear points!'

'Great idea!' they chorused, laughing.

At the same time as the boys were weighing up their title chances Mr Kenning was receiving the good news he'd been hoping for that might help them to achieve that success. Mr Turner, the Headmaster, had just informed him that a new boy would be joining his class after the Christmas

holidays – his name was Alan Clayton!

Alan's power and skill would be sure to strengthen the squad, but for the moment Mr Kenning decided to keep the new arrival a secret from the boys – at least until after the Fullerton Cup-tie.

But there was bad news too. Ricky was under doctor's orders to rest his arm for a few weeks, and that meant strictly no football! Robin Tainton, however, had grown considerably in confidence during the week's practices, and the team knew they could rely on him not to let anyone down. He was determined to do his very best.

The teacher's main job in class that week was to keep the footballers' minds on their work, and stop them dreaming about the approaching big game. 'Work hard and play hard,' he reminded them. 'But concentrate on one thing at a time.'

He chose the team on Thursday as usual.

Team v. Fullerton –
2nd round of Frisborough Trophy:

Robin Tainton
Jimmy McDowell   Scott Peters   Andrew Fisher   Paul Curtis
John Robinson   Jeff Thompson (*capt*)   Graham Ford
David Woodward   Gary Clarke   Dale Gregson
Subs: Ian Freeman, Dean Walters

Graham had justified his new position with that great second-half display against St John's, playing just behind the front three as an extra roaming attacker.

'We simply threw it away against Fullerton in that League game,' admitted Jeff at Friday's team meeting.

'We were 2-0 up after about ten minutes, got all big-headed and so lost 4-2,' moaned Jimmy. 'Ridiculous!'

'Well, we promised it wouldn't happen again, and it won't. No easing up this time,' said Scott.

'I'm glad you all remember that,' said Mr Kenning. 'But they're still a good strong side, and they've only lost to Fairway so far this season. It should be a great game and I wish you luck. It's also the last match before the end of term so let's try and finish with a good performance.'

He repeated the words of encouragement as the team took the field the next morning at Fullerton School, eager for action in the cold, damp air. He saw Jeff give Robin a special pat on the back, and he crossed his fingers that the lad would play as well as he could.

Both sides began forcefully, looking for an early vital breakthrough. The tall Fullerton forwards soon made their presence felt again, proving quite a handful to keep in check. Whenever one of the Sandford defenders went in to make a tackle, the others had to provide support and cover in case the attacker managed to barge through the first challenge.

After a slightly nervous start, when he fumbled a well-struck back pass from Paul, Robin became more sure of himself with the help of two good saves in quick succession. He was quite sturdily built for his age and was not in the least daunted by the big opponents. He positioned himself well, usually handled cleanly, and the team soon realized with relief that he was capable of looking after himself.

Fullerton just about had the edge in the first half, playing better football than before, but no goals came, and Sandford steadily looked more dangerous as halftime approached. David was having little joy against a quick-tackling full back, and consequently most of their attacks were worked down the left by Graham and Dale, who were pleased to be back in full partnership again.

Graham came the closest to scoring. He picked up a clearance from Andrew,

neatly exchanged passes with Dale, and then hared towards goal chased by two defenders. He was noted for his powerful shooting, and as the keeper came out he hit a beauty from twenty metres. The rocketing ball flew past the keeper's groping hands and pounded against the crossbar with a tremendous thwack before rebounding out of play, leaving the bar vibrating and Graham with only the generous applause of the spectators for consolation.

Then just as the whistle sounded Robin

managed to cling on to a stinger from close range. So the teams were still level.

'Well played, boys,' Mr Kenning encouraged during the brief break. 'Try this half to put the pressure on them more often – you're tending to back off, giving them too much time and space to move forward. Keep challenging all the while.'

'We can beat them now,' spoke up Jeff, voicing the team's thoughts. 'We can do it, I'm sure.'

'Right then. Go out and enjoy it and show us. Do what you have to do.'

And they certainly tried. They surprised Fullerton with their inspired attacks: Dale had two good shots at goal, and John then fastened on to a loose ball to fire one only just wide.

But there was still no goal, and suddenly without warning a long clearance caught Sandford's defence stretched, Scott and Andrew stranded too far upfield, leaving two forwards loose and heading for goal. Jimmy desperately chased across to challenge but just when it appeared he might succeed, the attacker flicked the ball to his teammate who went clear.

A goal seemed certain, but Robin came off his line like an express train. The big forward had to decide quickly whether to shoot or try to dribble round the advancing keeper. At speed it is rarely as simple as it looks. For a split second he hesitated and took his eye off the ball, and in that vital moment Robin pounced and flung himself sideways at his feet. He smothered the ball and his opponent went tumbling over him, knocking the breath out of both of them.

The referee stopped the game to check they were OK, but Robin was too winded to fully appreciate the clapping and congratulations he was receiving from the touchline and his friends. He got to his

feet, and only then did Mr Kenning see that Robin still had the ball firmly in his grasp! He had to smile with admiration at the youngster's pluckiness.

This inspiration to the team was rewarded quickly when the deadlock was at last broken. David lost the ball in a tackle but it ran for Jeff, who curled it into the middle. Gary and a defender both missed it and Dale popped up behind them strangely unmarked. He didn't have time to think as it skidded to him, but he coolly guided it first time to the keeper's right and into the corner of the goal.

Sandford's celebrations, however, were cut short by Jeff organizing them back into their positions. 'No relaxing,' he bellowed. 'C'mon, let's get at them again.'

From the restart, believing that actions speak louder than words, Jeff tackled very strongly and strode away with the ball, leaving his opponent gingerly to pick himself up off the floor.

But despite all their efforts they couldn't add to their score, and disappointingly Gary had faded right out of the game after a useful first half. The teacher wondered whether Gary might be overanxious about making mistakes if he

played his natural game and tried to do too much on his own. Gary's behaviour was still a bit of a mystery.

'Best to bring him off, and hope he's back on song properly after the holiday,' he thought.

Ian was sent on, Graham moved back up to centre-forward and Gary came over to stand forlornly and quietly next to Dean. Graham was soon in the thick of the action, putting a half-chance just over the bar. But a one-goal lead is never safe enough.

Five minutes from the end the Fullerton right winger sent a low centre into the area which Andrew half cleared. But it was crashed back into the crowded box and Robin only saw it very late. He blocked it well but wasn't able to hold on to it, and the loose ball was gleefully cracked home from point-blank range for the equalizer.

They were back to square one, and could scarcely believe it. But Jimmy with his infectious enthusiasm spurred them on again. 'C'mon, let's get started, we won't score standing here looking at each other.' He picked up the ball and hoofed it defiantly back up to the centre circle.

The lads responded, and knowing time was running out, Jeff told Ian to stay deep to allow Scott and any other defender more freedom to join in the attacks without leaving any gaps. Mr Kenning was pleased to see them working things out for themselves on the pitch. Jeff was out to win, not to draw, and was prepared to take risks now in the Cup to achieve it. This time luck was on Sandford's side, and the simple tactical switch worked like a dream.

With only a minute remaining they forced a corner on the right. David swung it in for John to touch on, but it was cleared away and seemingly out of danger. But Scott was standing where there would normally have been a space. He had

advanced right up, safe in the knowledge that Ian was covering behind him. The ball dropped invitingly at his feet, begging to be leathered back. He had time carefully to set his sights, draw back his right foot and let fly with all his might, remembering to keep his body over the ball to ensure it stayed low.

His arms were raised in the air even before the ball smacked against the back of the net between the goalie and the defender on the line. Scott's very first goal for the school, and what a time to do it! It had won the Cup-tie and he felt like a hero as his teammates ran to congratulate him. He'd been dreaming of a moment like this for years!

Fullerton's spirited fight-back was in vain. The final whistle was blown soon afterwards and the excellent match came to an end.

'Semi-Finals now next term,' Mr Kenning announced as he toured the happy changing area, praising each of the lads in turn for their performance. Robin's face glowed with pride and pleasure, and even Gary was joining in with the fun.

'Keep practising during the holidays,' he continued as they were all dressed and about ready to leave, and then added with a smile, 'Don't eat too many mince pies or Christmas pud or you'll be too fat to play!'

He pretended that he had just thought of something. 'Oh yes, one more thing. Remember the tall fair-haired Kelworth lad in that other Cup match?'

'We sure do!' replied Jeff as everyone nodded. 'Who could forget him? His heading was magic.'

'Yes, and we've got to tackle him again in the League,' groaned Scott in mock horror.

Mr Kenning laughed. 'No you won't, Scott, he's left them.'

'Phew, that's good news,' said Andrew. 'I wouldn't like to meet him again!'

'I'm afraid you'll have to play against him lots of times,' the teacher grinned, highly amused. 'In practice!'

'You don't mean . . .' breathed Jeff, catching on.

'I do. Alan Clayton is moving to Sandford, and he'll be your new teammate next term.'

There was a general gasp of stunned amazement before an excited babble broke out amongst them as the realization sunk in.

'That is really something,' enthused Jeff loudly. 'Incredible. Just great!'

7 Winter Tactics

The Christmas holidays quickly slipped away; busy, happy days with lots of new things to do and enjoy. But at least the footballers didn't mind returning to school afterwards!

'Hiya, Jeff,' called Jimmy. 'Have a good holiday?'

'Pretty good. Can't wait to get cracking with soccer again though.'

'That's all you think about,' joked Paul. 'You were out playing on the park nearly all the time.'

Jeff was about to answer the jibe when Scott arrived breathlessly. 'You're all keen, aren't you? I thought I'd be the first here at this time. Have you told them yet, Jeff?'

'Told them what?' he teased.

'Told them what?' Scott repeated, mimicking Jeff's voice. 'About Alan of

103

course, that's what! We played football
yesterday . . .'

'Well that's not unusual,' broke in Paul
with a grin. 'You two would be playing
on the park at night as well if they had
floodlights there.'

'Shut up a minute and listen. Alan came
along and joined in, so we've become mates
already.'

Jeff picked up the story now. 'He's
tremendous, he really is. He knocked in
loads past Ricky. We'll be unbeatable now
he's with us!'

Alan Clayton soon became popular after
the usual shy start settling in to a new,
unfamiliar school, and he was made to
feel very welcome by the other children.
He loved football almost as much as Jeff
did, and he could hardly wait to have
the chance of playing for Sandford. He
remembered how good they were in the
Cup game, when he had scored the only

goal against them. But in two weeks' time, if he was picked, his début would be in the home League match against his old friends of Kelworth, and he relished the prospect.

In the first lunchtime practice of term it was obvious that the forwards especially were trying even harder to impress than usual, hoping not to lose their place in the team. Alan's arrival would certainly keep everyone on their toes.

'We'll have to play our best all the time,' said Dale as they were changing afterwards.

'It's a strong squad now,' replied Jeff. 'Two good keepers and plenty of competition for all the other places too.'

Robin was pleased to hear that Jeff thought so highly of him. Even Ricky, fully fit again, was secretly rather anxious after being told about Robin's promising displays.

'That's the trouble,' joked David, 'too much competition. Sorry, Alan, you'll have to go back, there's no room for you here.'

They all laughed, but Graham shouted out over all the noise. 'Well, I'm still top scorer. Six goals in the League. Who else has got some?'

'Big-head!' laughed David. 'I'm only one behind you.'

'Jeff and me have three each,' joined in John, 'and we're only in midfield.'

'Four for me, counting the Cup,' chirped up Dale.

Jimmy checked the noticeboard where all the match details were recorded. 'Paul and Dean have scored in the League,' he read out. 'Plus one own goal. And . . . er . . . David, Gary and Scott have also scored in the Cup.'

'What a goal, the winner!' shouted Scott, and he was immediately showered with socks and shirts.

'Anyway, it doesn't matter who scores them,' finished Jeff as the lunch bell sounded, 'as long as we keep banging them in. And now we've got Alan here to help us. It's all about good teamwork.'

But the boys were in for a disappointment. Just before the Saturday of the game it snowed, and then froze solid overnight. After inspecting the bone hard, icy pitch Mr Kenning had no option but to cancel the match.

'Sorry, lads, it's much too dangerous. This is winter soccer for you. You can't guarantee to play fixtures when arranged.'

He went off to telephone Kelworth in the hope of fixing it up for the next week instead.

'I used to enjoy the snow,' complained Jimmy, 'but not any more. Not when it wrecks our football, anyway!'

'Even slides and snowballs can't make up for it,' agreed Scott.

'Perhaps it will thaw out by next Saturday,' said Jeff optimistically. 'I can't wait to get at them again.'

'Who?' asked Andrew.

'Anybody. Just anybody!'

Indeed, despite the very cold weather and some frost, the situation was more hopeful the following week.

'I think the pitch will be playable as long as the weather doesn't worsen,' said Mr Kenning at a team meeting for the re-arranged Kelworth game. 'You've already played in clinging mud, and now you'll have the experience of a hard, slippery surface where it's difficult to turn quickly without falling over.'

'As long as we can play I'm not bothered what the ground is like,' put in Jeff. 'It's the same for both teams.'

'True. But we can gain an extra advantage by wearing training shoes instead of football boots. They're better for playing on frozen grounds where studs can't grip.'

Ricky was back in goal to his delight, and Robin was content to know that his turn for a regular place was still to come next year. With Alan at centre-forward and Graham linking up down the left, there was sadly no place for Gary, who joined Ian as substitute. Mr Kenning hoped very much that Gary would soon be back to his brilliant if erratic best so that he could include him again somewhere in the side.

Graham was enjoying his new position more and more as it involved him in defence and in attack. It was all action, and of course he was still scoring goals.

The match went ahead as expected on a frosty white pitch, tricky but not impossible. Sandford were well equipped for the conditions, all wearing trainers to help them keep their footing better, except for Gary who didn't own a pair and hadn't bothered to borrow any. Kelworth,

however, were not so well prepared, and most of their team would soon be sliding around.

Alan Clayton was naturally keyed up to do well against his former chums. In the joking beforehand they vowed he wouldn't get a touch, while he boasted to them he'd probably score about ten! It was a strange feeling to be playing against them so soon after leaving, but he very much wanted to help beat them.

And they couldn't have had a better start. Inside two minutes, before either team had properly warmed up, Sandford went a goal ahead. The clumsy defender who had fouled Gary so badly in the Cup-tie slipped attempting a clearance. Dale, nipping nimbly round him in his trainers, took full advantage and slid the ball neatly past the diving keeper's left hand.

Sandford skated around after that, enjoying their first taste of real winter soccer, forgetting about the cold, and not minding too much when they fell over sometimes. Even the Kelworth lads in boots gradually adjusted to the surface, but they never moved as freely or as confidently as the others.

There were plenty of unavoidable mistakes but they soon learned to hit long balls for the forwards to run on to, as defenders found it difficult to turn. They let the ball do more of the work, playing it simply and not attempting too much on their own. Easy, straightforward passes were best rather than running too far with the ball and losing control.

Jeff was a tower of strength in the middle, dominating the game, spraying passes out to both wings and down the centre for Alan. For big lads they were both doing remarkably well, as mostly it was the smaller, better balanced boys who coped more comfortably in such conditions.

When Kelworth did manage their first

real shot Ricky got down well, getting his body behind an awkward skidding effort.

'Well saved!' praised Scott. 'Welcome back.'

'Better than being cold standing here watching you lot run about,' he replied after kicking the ball away.

Alan won a corner just before half-time. And from David's cross he himself jumped high at the near post and glanced the ball with his forehead, but unfortunately it struck the woodwork and deflected out.

'Hard luck!' consoled Jeff, helping him up. 'You'll get a goal, don't worry.'

He did too – with his next touch! The goalkeeper slipped and sliced his kick straight to John who controlled it well and pushed it back straightaway before the defence could recover. Alan was on to it like a flash, and boomed it into the bulging net with great elation before being swamped by his delighted new teammates.

'Great game,' praised Jeff at the break. 'Just keep it up, everybody.'

'That's right,' continued Mr Kenning, 'keep it simple. Play the way you're facing, and let the ball run.'

The second half followed a similar pattern, with Sandford emphasizing their undoubted superiority. They took no risks in defence and allowed the visitors few shooting chances. At the other end David and Jeff saw shots skid wide, and their keeper saved well from Alan. But more goals were inevitable.

Graham capped a fine display with a powerfully struck goal, and then Dale's second made it 4-0 when he clipped home a smart pass from John ten minutes from time. The little winger was probably the best balanced player on the pitch, and had whipped past his full back at will, giving him a nightmare morning.

Both substitutes were able to sample

113

the conditions and stop their shivers on the line, David and Paul making way for them. The teacher tried to use the subs whenever possible, but often their mere presence made those on the field keep trying their hardest in order to stay on. The subs were important, whether they actually kicked a ball or not.

Ian settled in fine at full back but Gary in his boots just slithered around. A scoring chance did in fact come his way, and one which on a normal day would have presented no difficulties, but this time as he stretched to reach it his other foot slipped from underneath him and he collapsed in a heap. He was cross, but managed to see the funny side of it later when he was ribbed by the others about his footwear.

In the end everyone was glad to return to the warmth of the school building for a very welcome hot drink.

'We missed Alan's power up front,' sighed

Kelworth's teacher. 'You'll take some stopping now with Alan there.'

Mr Kenning looked across with satisfaction to his team. 'I must admit I'm optimistic. You have to be with such a marvellous bunch of lads, but there's a long way to go yet – anything could happen.'

The winter weather continued to play all its tricks, and it was difficult to arrange practices let alone matches. But eventually it cleared up sufficiently to allow the next League game to go ahead, away at Scotney School.

The pitch looked sticky in places, but the main problems were going to be caused by the strong, blustery winds down the length of the ground. Scotney were not reputed to be one of the better sides, but the teacher repeated his warnings about expecting an easy win. 'Football's a funny game; nothing is ever certain, and you've

never won or lost a game until the final whistle. Always play hard right to the end.'

The team was unchanged, except that young Sammy King replaced Ian as substitute to gain useful experience for the future, as he looked a fine prospect.

It was a cold February morning, and they found themselves facing the full force of the wind. Whenever possible they were sensible enough to try to keep the ball on the ground to stop the wind catching it and blowing it back towards them again. They played mostly short passes out of defence, the forwards dropping deeper to pick them up, as attempted long clearances made little impression against the wind.

Scotney naturally strived to make good use of this, and one shot in particular was given extra venom by the wind. It swirled viciously towards the corner of the goal before Ricky dived full length to turn it miraculously away.

'Save of the season!' applauded Jeff running to him. 'Brilliant, Ricky.'

It was a vital save too, preventing them from falling behind, and gradually their better footballing ability began to show through. They ran well for each other, moving into space close by in support and calling for the ball when in a good position, and their passing was impressively accurate.

They constructed several scoring opportunities and made what use they could of the wind, hitting the ball hard to their forwards on the attack so that the wind would hold it up for them and allow them to reach it comfortably.

After a few near misses they finally succeeded. Jeff turned the ball out to David who ran straight at the full back, suddenly swerved to send him off balance and then zoomed past him. As he neared the penalty area, he passed inside to Alan

to avoid a tackle and managed to keep going for the quick return. Lunging forward and almost stumbling, he was just able to flick the ball past the advancing goalie for a thoroughly deserved lead.

Scotney desperately threw more players forward but Ricky's defenders were in good form and, despite being hard pressed, appeared to be holding out. But then suddenly a snap shot caught them out and the scores were level as they all stopped for a breather at half-time.

'Now let's see what we can do with this wind in our favour,' said Mr Kenning to the flushed youngsters. 'Be careful not to overhit it or you'll never catch it. Make them do the chasing, keep them stretched. Use the wings, boys,' he urged as they trooped back on. 'Spread it wide and you'll run them ragged.'

They intended to do just that and they soon displayed their full attacking force, leaving Scotney's brave triers breathless and leg-weary by the end. The home team found it very difficult to clear their own lines, and Ricky was scarcely troubled, except by the cold!

It was surprising that they only scored three more and didn't run the total into double figures. A mixture of bad luck, hurried shooting and good goalkeeping accounted for it, and the awkward wind would balloon shots up over the bar unless the striker kept well over the ball as he hit it. But they all thoroughly enjoyed themselves.

Everyone managed a shot at goal, and even a long, bouncing kick from Ricky almost caused a goal as players scrambled for it in the area. Graham hit the post twice, but Alan put one of the rebounds in for the second goal. With David and Dale running free down the flanks Scotney pulled virtually all their players back to

pack their defence, and managed somehow to block many goal-bound efforts.

Alan revelled in playing alongside such good players, and his next goal was a dream. Receiving the ball on the edge of the area, he sidestepped one challenge and immediately let fly with his right foot. The ball came bouncing back out of the net before anyone else had moved.

John and Andrew now gave way to allow Gary and Sammy to join in the fun, and the fourth and final goal gave Mr Kenning a lot of pleasure. It was Gary's first League goal, just three minutes from time.

Jeff and Alan had seen their shots charged down, and the ball came out to the substitute on the right. As everyone shouted for a centre with three defenders between him and the goal, Gary did his own very special thing. It was as if he had been waiting for this moment to show what he could really do.

He calmly put his foot on the ball, looked up, assessed the situation instantly and invited the first challenge. The nearest defender lunged in, but the ball had gone, whipped deftly away by Gary's left foot. He then cut in, gathered speed and jinked past the next two tackles. He was almost knocked over but he kept his balance and finally screwed the ball through the narrowest of gaps between the keeper, the post and a player on the line.

Gary threw his arms up in delight at his supreme individualist goal, and the others ran over to congratulate him in amazement.

It had been a very entertaining 4-1 victory with some excellent goals, and nobody had ever seen Gary so happy. Often inclined to be rather quiet and brooding, he was laughing as loudly as anyone in the boisterous changing room.

'Who can I possibly leave out now for

our game with Little Beaton?' the teacher wondered with a smile on his way home. 'They're all playing so well.'

But that happy problem was soon to be resolved in a most unexpected way. It was to prove more of a question of who could possibly play in order to field a full side! Illness was about to strike; and if they were ever going to catch Tanby at the top of the League they could not afford to slip up now!

8 Struck Down

Everything went well until the end of the week. The high winds had dropped, and all the boys were eagerly anticipating the Little Beaton game.

That was before the troubles began. By Friday the classrooms were half-empty as children were struck down one by one by an influenza virus sweeping the village.

Mr Kenning called an emergency play-time meeting to survey the wreckage of his first-team squad. The prospects looked bleak as the casualty list numbered Jimmy, Scott, Graham, David, Alan, Dale, Dean and Robin.

'Whatever happens,' he stressed to the remainder, 'we're going ahead with this game if we possibly can. We'll have to make up a team with lads from the reserve squad – it will be a good chance for them at least.'

'We'll just have to play twice as hard,' said a determined Jeff.

'It'll show the others we don't need them!' grinned Andrew.

'I'll check round to see who's still fit, and then we'll just have to hope that those chosen will still be healthy tomorrow morning. Otherwise we'll really be in trouble!'

'Lucky we're at home,' said Jeff afterwards to Ricky. 'We can always go and drag somebody out of bed if we're one short!'

The goalkeeper laughed at the thought. 'Perhaps spectators should bring their boots along just in case – they may get a game!'

The boys in the other practice group, mostly younger ones, had been making good progress and showed promising skills. They had plenty of enthusiasm, but still had a lot to learn in many ways. Some of these players were found to be away too, but in the end the teacher managed to

formulate a rather odd looking team with several unfamiliar names down to make an unexpected school team début.

All eyes were on the noticeboard at lunchtime.

Team v. Little Beaton:

	Ricky Collier		
Lee Robinson	Sammy King	Andrew Fisher	Paul Curtis
John Robinson	Jeff Thompson *(capt)*		Philip Bates
Robert Jackson	Gary Clarke		Ian Freeman

Subs: Simon Henderson, Colin Allsop

The newcomers were sure to try as hard as they possibly could, and that was all that anyone could ask of them. It would be very interesting to see how they performed, supported by the hard core of regulars around them, and it would be great experience for them.

Substitute Colin Allsop was a sturdy nine-year-old who had a good eye for goal, and Lee was thrilled about playing along-side John again, as in the Sevens. Two boys in Year Five, Robert and Philip, deserved their chance: Robert was a nippy winger whilst left-footed Philip preferred coming forward from midfield but tended to wander around a little too much.

The reliable Ian was pleased to have a go in attack for a change, and sub Simon Henderson, an older lad in Mrs Cowper's class, was absolutely delighted to be included. He was really keen and never missed a practice, and this was a reward for his boundless enthusiasm which compensated for some of the skills that he lacked.

Perhaps the most remarkable fact was that Gary was still at school. This time last year, whether ill or not, he would almost certainly have used all these absences as an excuse to have a few days off himself as well. But thanks to football his outlook had apparently changed – he obviously didn't want to miss the match!

Fortunately they all reported to school fit and well the following morning. But then Mr Kenning saw Jeff, who was sitting in the changing area with his head down. He sat up, putting on a brave front as the teacher approached, but his face looked pale. 'Oh no,' thought Mr Kenning. 'The bug's even claimed him.'

Then out loud he said, 'You look as though you should be at home in bed, Jeff.'

'My parents are away this weekend. My aunt's looking after me and she said I could come.'

'I'm not sure it's wise. How do you feel?'

'OK at the moment; I'll be all right. I want to play.'

Although against his better judgement, the teacher didn't have the heart to refuse him. 'I'll let you start the match, but if I see you're struggling we'll have you off. Understand?'

Jeff nodded, his face brightening up, and feeling better already. Half his worries had been the thought of not being allowed to play.

The visitors could scarcely conceal their delight when they arrived and heard the tale of woe. Having expected a beating, they suddenly began to fancy their chances against such a depleted team.

'We'll lick you now,' taunted one of them just before the start. 'That'll stop you winning the League.'

'Rubbish!' retorted Ian. 'We'd still beat you hopping about on one leg, you'll see.'

Mr Kenning wished them luck and told them to enjoy the game, whatever the result, but there was nothing more he could do.

Little Beaton swung straight into the attack down the right, the winger going past Philip who failed to tackle strongly enough. The centre-forward was quickest to the centre but Ricky was alert and saved his shot well down at the near post.

'C'mon, defence, get to the ball,' yelled Jeff. 'Mark goal-side, Sammy, between them and the goal all the time.'

They were pressed back for this opening spell of the game, but Jeff was holding them together, organizing and helping those around him. He looked his usual dynamic self at the moment, enjoying the extra challenge.

Andrew scrambled a shot away off the line and they conceded several corners, at times having to be content with clearing their lines hurriedly. Only Gary remained permanently upfield, appearing rather desolate as the lone striker.

Ricky made more good saves, but had a piece of luck when after Jeff had blocked a shot, the rebound was sliced to one side. It beat him, but with relief he saw it strike the post and run to safety.

'Phew, that was too close for comfort,' he sighed.

'Well left, Ricky,' joked Andrew. 'Good judgement!'

Young Lee was having a terrific duel with his winger, both about the same height, but with two years' age difference between them. He was showing up well, and also linking splendidly with his brother on the right hand side.

The first time that Robert Jackson, playing ahead of them, had a chance to run with the ball he whisked it away past one defender quite cleverly, but then lost it to

the next who was backing up.

'Don't push it so far in front of you,' advised Mr Kenning as he came alongside. 'Keep it under closer control.'

But as the winger began to show some nice touches, Philip Bates had rather drifted out of the game. He was rarely where he should have been, and was chasing the ball instead of letting it come to him.

It was only when Jeff and John occasionally found space to come forward that Sandford looked more like themselves. One such attack allowed Ian to have a fine effort turned round the post. From the corner Gary slipped very neatly past two defenders but could only blast the ball into the side netting.

No goals by half-time, and the game was still in the balance thanks to good, solid defensive work. The teacher congratulated them. 'Keep it up, it could go our way yet.

You'd see more of the ball, Philip, if you stayed in your proper position. Well tried, but we'll give Simon a chance this half.'

As Simon Henderson peeled off his track-suit like lightning, Mr Kenning asked Jeff how he felt.

'Fine. I'm OK.' But strain showed on his face.

His teacher wasn't convinced. The boy had been playing well, but was probably taxing himself to the limit. He decided to substitute him before very long.

They restarted with fresh hopes but almost immediately disaster befell them. Ricky slightly mis-hit a goal kick, and the ball was quickly knocked back into the area. There was a terrific scramble on the six-yard line where Paul, Sammy and Simon all tried unsuccessfully to clear it before the ball was poked agonizingly out of Ricky's reach by their winger – they were now one goal down.

'C'mon, lads,' said John. 'We gave them that. Now we'll have to score two ourselves.'

But they had to withstand a lot more pressure first as the visitors went all-out for another goal to sew it up. At times they had to clear desperately, but often they showed great skill and composure by playing the ball out purposefully.

Jeff was beginning to flag, and the teacher called on Colin Allsop to take his place. Though he would never admit it, Jeff was feeling pretty awful.

'No more,' consoled Mr Kenning as he led him off. 'You've done enough. We'll have to manage without you now, I'm afraid.'

He allowed him to stay and watch till the end. 'But then straight back to bed or you'll be off school for a long time.'

Almost as though Jeff's departure was a kind of signal that they must raise their own game to compensate, the team seemed to buzz around with even more life and determination to get back into the match.

Especially Gary Clarke. He really began to turn on his skills. The whole team was fed up with defending and sensed that the mood had changed. There was nothing to lose, and they put Little Beaton to the test. The quick, lively Colin played up alongside Gary, and this unlikely twosome somehow clicked together.

John assumed the captaincy and drove them forward, and incredibly it was now Sandford doing most of the attacking. Whether their opponents had decided to sit back and hold their lead, or had been caught unawares by this sudden revival, it was hard to say, but the transformation was remarkable.

Paul once found the opportunity to come through and have a crack, the ball just whistling over the bar. Simon battled away eagerly down the left with Ian and performed rather better than anticipated. The

new boys were carried along as the team hit form, and Mr Kenning was delighted and surprised, having thought the game lost when Jeff went off.

But, with time running out, goals wouldn't come. Robert cut in dangerously from the right and swerved a shot narrowly wide with Little Beaton's previous teamwork in ruins.

It was finally, however, to be Gary's day. As he saw more of the ball his confidence returned and he was willing to try anything from solo runs to rapid passing movements, and he produced all kinds of cheeky, subtle touches to deceive opponents. Twice the keeper saved well from him. One shot was cleared off the line, and then five minutes from the end a tremendous effort hit the crossbar. It was all very frustrating.

A shot from John skimmed across the line and stayed out, and nothing ever seemed likely to go in until John again lofted a hopeful centre into the area. It was beaten out, but Gary doubled back to take it off Andrew's toes, jinked past one challenge and found himself just inside the penalty area and faced by two opponents.

Suddenly, without warning, he flicked the ball up into the air and, as the defenders gawped, hit it on the volley

with his right foot as it came down.

'Sheer magic!' was all Jeff could say to describe it later as he remembered the ball looping up then dipping down into the top far corner of the net behind a bewildered, stranded goalkeeper. Unstoppable; and Gary was completely engulfed by excited teammates. Jeff almost ran on to the field himself to join in.

Even then there was still enough time to see more drama at both ends. To their credit Little Beaton broke away before Sandford had properly calmed down but they were rescued by Ricky who had remained alert for danger. Goalkeepers

know all about the agonies of letting in late goals, and he made sure he didn't make a mistake this time. He booted the ball far downfield without ceremony to be chased by Colin and Robert. The winger touched it on, and the young substitute had a split second to shoot before he was tackled. He even thought he'd scored an incredible winner, but the touchline shouts were mistaken – it was the side netting, only centimetres wide.

Amidst all the noise the final whistle sounded, leaving both sides exhausted and happy to share the points at 1-1.

'Marvellous game,' the Little Beaton sportsmaster said to Mr Kenning as the boys cheered each other off. 'I'm certainly glad we didn't have to play you at full strength!' He grinned and added, 'For a while there I thought we were going to beat you and cause another surprise.'

'Another? What do you mean?'

'You haven't heard yet?' Well don't be disappointed with today's draw – it's not all that crucial.'

'Come on, don't keep me in suspense,' laughed Mr Kenning.

'OK, I'll tell you straight! Tanby have lost at last – 2-1 to Fullerton.'

Heartened by the good news he went in to congratulate the boys for their spirited display and recovery. 'You did yourselves and the school proud today, all of you. Well done!'

'But we've fallen further behind Tanby now, though,' said Andrew rather glumly.

'You're wrong there, Andrew. No need to worry. Tanby have been beaten by . . .'

The players didn't wait for any further explanation – they celebrated with a huge cheer which drowned and deafened everything and everybody else in the room!

9 Cup Clash with Tanby

School returned to normal the next week as the children filtered back after recovery, but Jeff didn't appear until Wednesday. He was just in time for the week's main practice – as well he knew of course! Nothing was going to prevent him from taking part in the Cup preparations.

'What a game last week!' he enthused as they changed. 'The whole team played great, the new ones too.'

'We played even better without you!' joked Ian.

Jeff laughed and shoved him playfully. 'You had to. I can't look after you all the time!'

'Gary was fantastic near the end,' John told all those who had missed it, for the hundredth time since Monday.

'So we've heard,' groaned Graham. 'I

believe you. It's a pity he can't do it all the time, though.'

'And now *he's* away this week,' reported Jimmy. 'I saw him last night. He reckons his mum is keeping him off to do some jobs for her.'

'He'll be back for the Cup match this Saturday, never fear,' said John confidently. 'We're going to need a full-strength team for that.'

'What a Semi-Final!' exclaimed Jeff, becoming excited already. 'Tanby at home. Superb. It'll be just like the Final itself.'

'They'll be out for revenge after their Sevens defeat by us too,' added Scott. 'We'll have to disappoint them!'

'You'll have to do it without me you know, I'm afraid.' The words were Alan's, who had been sitting quietly at the edge of the group, thinking.

'What do you mean?' asked Jimmy. 'You're not moving again, are you?'

'No, of course not, but you've already knocked me out, remember? I'll be Cup-tied, I suppose, just like professional footballers are when they change clubs.'

The others groaned now that they realized the possibility for the first time. Mr Kenning confirmed it at the practice too. 'I'm afraid that's right, lads, I've checked already. No Alan this Saturday again to help us.'

They tried to make light of it but they all knew that it would make their task even harder.

'Let's hope that Gary will still be on top form to make up for it anyway,' said Jeff. 'I bet they'll remember how well he played against them in the Sevens Semi-Final for the 'B' team. They won't be looking forward to meeting him again!'

With everybody fit again the team was back to normal with Gary chosen as centre-forward, despite his continued absence. He did return, however, on Friday and made a dash for the noticeboard, delighted to see his name still in the team. But Mrs Cowper, his class teacher, had other ideas.

She broke the bad news to Mr Kenning in the staffroom at playtime. 'I'm sorry, but I'm fed up with that Gary. He had no decent excuse for being away, and he's falling further and further behind with his work, so I've given him a lot of work to take home this weekend.'

Mr Kenning began to suspect what was coming next.

'He's thinking more about his football than his lessons, so I've told him straight. No more football until he tries harder and does better work!'

Mr Kenning was dismayed, and although he understood Mrs Cowper's viewpoint, he did make a protest on Gary's behalf: but to no avail. Gary needed encouragement to improve, not the kind of punishment which

stopped him doing something that he was good at, and that boosted his confidence. This was a real setback just when the boy had seemed to be coming on well.

In the end it was agreed that they should see how the rest of the day went, and whether Gary could redeem himself. He did work harder, but resentfully and dejected at the prospect of the ban, and he took little interest in what he was doing, making many mistakes in the process.

Mrs Cowper wasn't satisfied, and decided to carry out her threat. During the afternoon's art and craft session there was a knock on Mr Kenning's classroom door, and in trailed a pale-looking Gary Clarke.

The footballers looked up from their painting and modelling in concern, guessing the worst from the boy's expression.

His eyes reddened, he blurted out that he wasn't allowed to play, and then stood motionless staring at the floor.

144

'I know all about it, Gary, and I've spoken up for you,' explained the teacher. He held the tearful face up. 'We all want you back in the team, but you must show Mrs Cowper how well you can do in class too. Then everything will soon be all right again. Agreed?'

Gary nodded, then turned and hurried out of the room and into the cloakroom opposite. Mr Kenning thought about calling him back, but it was best to let him cry out his disappointment in private.

Jeff and the others looked equally upset.

'Robert Jackson can play instead,' Mr Kenning said, 'and we'll have Ian and Colin as subs.'

David moved inside to the centre to allow Robert to play on the wing, as Graham Ford now preferred to stay in his new position down the left side. Even without Gary and Alan the Sandford boys were determined to succeed and they assembled on a glorious

February morning with the sun shining and conditions ideal for the time of year.

What a dream start Sandford enjoyed too! After early skirmishes around both goals in front of a large gathering of parents and supporters, Jeff hit a long pass out to find Dale on the left wing. Eager for action he took on the full back and whistled past him on the outside. His cross was blocked but the ball rebounded to him, and this time he simply rolled it inside into the path of Graham who was steaming up alongside.

He steadied himself, and before he could be tackled, hammered a well-aimed power drive wide of the despairing lunge of Kevin Baker, the Tanby keeper, and into the far corner.

'Great stuff!' yelled Jeff into his ear as they swarmed around the scorer. 'What a beauty!'

But of course it wasn't going to be that easy.

Ricky was forced to dive at the centre-forward's feet as he eluded Scott's close marking for the first time. Then he had to fling himself to his right to get behind a low, stinging shot from the wing.

'Well saved, Ricky,' shouted John. 'Come on, defence, give him some cover. Let's have these shots blocked.'

Tanby's left back appeared to be a possible weak link in their armour, and Robert was giving him a testing time. On one occasion he nipped around him and his centre was met well by David, but the ball just clipped the wrong side of the post.

Jeff almost made it 2-0 when he sent a dipping shot skidding centimetres wide, but Sandford weren't able to increase their lead. As the first half drew to a close, Tanby pressed hard and grabbed the crucial equalizer. Paul had cleared a shot for a corner, and from this the defenders were guilty of ball-watching and not marking

their opponents tightly enough. The ball
was glanced down for the scorer to stab
it home unchallenged past the helpless
Ricky.

It might have been easy to start blaming
each other, but as they gathered round for
the short rest Mr Kenning told them to forget about it. 'It's happened now, but that's
what does occur if you ease up and don't
watch where their players have moved to.
Stay goal-side of them.'

'They're very good,' breathed Jimmy
heavily, having had a difficult first half
against the speedy left winger.

'Yes, but so are we,' corrected Jeff. 'We
can beat them. C'mon, let's get at them
again.'

The second half began at the same cracking pace, with everyone present enjoying
the exciting end-to-end play. Ricky was
beaten again by one viciously curling shot,
but was lucky enough to see it rebound off

the inside of the post straight back into his grateful arms.

Then Kevin Baker made an excellent save from Dale, and was also in the right position to gather a cross from Graham safely and cleanly.

'He's going to take some beating again,' Graham said to Jeff.

'Yes, he's good, but we'll have to keep on trying. We won't score if we don't shoot!'

Tanby kept trying, too. Jimmy and Paul were playing well but were being stretched to the limit by the frequent raids down both flanks. Anything that did escape them, however, was firmly dealt with by Scott and Andrew in the middle. The minutes ticked by and the Cup-tie seemed destined for a replay.

Until, that is, the Tanby skipper Simon Walsh, breaking into Sandford's half, produced a moment of opportunism. His speed took him past John and then he shot unexpectedly on the run.

Ricky, well off his line, made a tremendous save low down to block the ball, but he failed to hold on to it. The ball rolled loose and as Scott and a Tanby forward tussled for it together it was the attacker who made the last important contact to send it bobbling into the net. 2-1 to Tanby, and they were rightly jubilant.

With time running out and the attack lacking the necessary vital spark to turn chances into goals, David moved back out wide to replace Robert, who was substituted by Colin Allsop to try to unsettle their defence. The youngster charged around enthusiastically, but their grip was now too strong.

Only once more did Sandford come close, despite Jeff's urgent driving and prompting, when David – looking happier on the wing – cut in past the left back and brought a good save out of Kevin.

It just wasn't to be their day, and no-one could deny Tanby their deserved victory. The schools were even now, one success each over the other, and the Tanby boys themselves had been mighty relieved when they realized that the substitute cyclist from the Sevens who had nearly upset them on his own was nowhere to be seen!

Although disappointed initially the boys accepted their defeat well which was very pleasing to Mr Kenning. By the time he joined them in the changing area, they had mostly recovered their outward spirits.

'Never mind, lads. Win or lose – in the end it's not that important. It's the way you play that matters, and you all played very well indeed. I'm proud of you.'

'We might still have won with Alan or Gary to help us,' said John, wistfully. 'I hope they can play in our League match against them.'

'It would have been great to have reached the Cup Final,' added Jeff. 'But now we haven't, we can go all out for the League instead.'

'Yes, that's even more special,' interrupted Scott, cheering up. 'It proves who's the best team over the whole season. That'll be the great final decider between us!'

10 Shooting Practice

Tuesday's practice session after school was thoroughly enjoyed as usual, the Cup defeat put well behind them in anticipation of the remaining two League games.

With Tanby School still a point ahead at the top, a good win against Gainsville Primary School on Saturday was vital if Sandford were to be in with a chance of the Championship in the final match of the season against their chief rivals.

They practised passing skills in small groups, keeping the ball away from opponents in a limited space which needed plenty of movement and good, quick control. Shooting practice followed, first from a centred ball, and then beating a defender before shooting at goal, where Ricky was in spectacular form.

Gary was there too, fortunately. He had

been absent the day before again, much to Mrs Cowper's annoyance. But the homework set had in fact been completed quite satisfactorily and she considered the punishment had been sufficient for the time being, especially after the team's result. The teacher had let him off with a stern lecture about his future work in the hope that from now on it would begin to improve.

Gary had perked up because of that, but even so he didn't look to Mr Kenning to be quite as sharp as he could be. He was still unpredictable and seemed to need some kind of challenge to inspire him, but hopefully his special skills would flourish when it mattered most.

Once, as he turned from fetching a ball from the fence behind the goal, a shot from Alan skimmed straight at him. Instinctively in one swift, easy movement he killed it on his instep, flicked it up and casually volleyed it back to Alan's feet.

Mr Kenning could only whistle softly to himself in admiration, doubting whether any of the boys, including Gary himself, fully appreciated the natural ability he had just demonstrated so brilliantly.

The session ended with their favourite game of attack against defence. Here the attack had to build up passing moves towards goal, scoring one point for a shot and three if they scored. The defenders had to try to break up these raids by good marking, covering, tackling and eventually aiming to clear the ball back over the halfway line to earn a point for themselves. This activity practised virtually all the situations they were likely to meet in a normal game and helped to strengthen understanding and improve general teamwork.

On this occasion, despite good resistance, the defence were trailing 6-8 when it neared the end of the practice. Then Ian worked the ball down the left to Graham,

and as Dale went on a decoy run wide to fool
Jimmy, Graham cut inside. He bustled past
Dean and slipped a pass to Alan between
Scott and Andrew. The blond striker shot
too hastily, but Jeff zoomed in to crash the
loose ball well out of Ricky's reach.

'Good goal. That's it, boys, for today, 11-6
to the attackers,' announced the teacher. 'I
can see Gainsville will have to watch out if
you're all on this form at the weekend!'

The team sheet went up on Thursday
with Alan restored at centre-forward, but
to Gary's disappointment he found he had
only been named as substitute along with
Sammy King. He rather felt that his recent
hard work in class deserved a place right
from the start!

A change did have to be made the next
day, however, but not to Gary's benefit.
Paul Curtis fell ill overnight and Sammy
was promoted to take his place at left
back. Paul's coolness and reliability might

have been sadly missed against stronger opposition, but Mr Kenning was confident that young Sammy would prove more than a capable replacement for this match. He was rapidly gaining experience and had the look of a future school team captain when his time came.

Saturday morning dawned fresh and clear and promised a typical, breezy March day. They were all extra keen to play well to ensure their place for the big Tanby game, knowing that there were players like Gary only too willing and able to step into their boots. For once, everything clicked into place perfectly, and they ran riot.

They found plenty of space for themselves by good, intelligent running off the ball, and even on Gainsville's smallish pitch they appeared to have metres to spare and often a wide choice of players to pass to. It was as though all the things that they had practised and worked at throughout the season

came off in splendid style. Even cheeky
back-heels and neat, quick one-twos were
succeeding against a slow-turning defence.

Dale and Alan soon put them two up,
and Ricky was a spectator for much of
the first half as the home team scarcely
managed to put a decent attacking move
together.

The two wingers were causing untold
confusion and danger, running almost free
against weak full backs. David it was, in
fact, who centred for his wing partner
Dale to stab home his own second goal.
Even Andrew Fisher saw a shot clunk
heavily against the crossbar.

Gainsville didn't have any nets on their
goals as all the other schools did, and
Graham was certain at half-time that a
shot of his that their teacher decided had
gone wide had indeed been a goal. The score
by then was 4-0 thanks to John.

'That's football, Graham,' said Mr

Kenning, curbing the boy's annoyance. 'You must accept the referee's decisions at all times, whether you agree or not. Maybe you're the one who's wrong, not him. Just forget it and get on with the game. These things happen – perhaps another time you may be given a goal which should have been disallowed!'

Graham nodded, not unduly upset because of the score, but he wanted one for himself all the same.

'What a great game!' grinned Jeff. 'We could get double figures at this rate.'

'Never mind about that,' said Scott surprisingly. 'Don't all go charging forward. We need defenders as well, you know.'

The opening minute proved Scott's point. The ball was suddenly booted away out of the Gainsville half and their centre-forward unexpectedly found himself in the clear with Sandford caught out of position. He was desperately chased by Scott and

Jimmy, but he kept his head and slotted the ball nicely past Ricky for their first goal.

'Now you see what can happen,' moaned Scott after picking the ball out of the hedge behind.

But even he soon cheered up as Sandford quickly reasserted their superior skills, and that goal remained Gainsville's only consolation. Sammy was never really tested and he performed well down the left side.

Dale gave a dance of delight as he claimed a hat-trick for himself and his team's fifth, and the team was playing so fluently that the use of the substitutes was delayed. They were really switching the ball about, the two wingers staying wide to avoid any bunching, and it was only the splendid efforts of Gainsville's goalkeeper that prevented the total mounting even more rapidly.

But after a neat exchange with David, Jeff capped a fine game with the sixth goal, hitting it just under the bar. To his relief, the referee gave it after a moment's careful consideration.

Reluctantly Mr Kenning called off John and Alan to allow Ian and Gary to join in the fun, but Gary was frustratingly subdued. 'Perhaps there's no stimulus for him, winning so easily,' the teacher pondered. 'I hope Tanby will satisfy his need for the right occasion to show off his skills!'

But the team continued to send in shots from every angle, and eventually Graham deservedly made it the highest score of the season, 7-1, right at the end. Ian's long range effort was blocked and Graham pounced on the ball, strode past two tired tackles and fired it home in determined fashion to make amends for the earlier one that got away.

Their keeper looked rather dejected as he trailed off, but Mr Kenning said a private word of praise to him for his performance

and the lad went into the school building with his head held high.

Sandford had probably produced their best football of the season in this match, which was the ideal preparation for the Tanby decider. Everyone was already very excited about that, although it was still a fortnight away. This was the best shooting practice they could have wished for!

Tanby were right on course for the Double, meeting Fairway in the Cup Final next Saturday, and then only Sandford would stand in their way for the League title too.

The top four schools in the League table with one match remaining appeared like this in the *Frisborough Journal:*

	P	W	D	L	F	A	Pts
Tanby	10	8	1	1	44	13	17
Sandford	10	7	2	1	38	12	16
Fairway	10	6	3	1	27	13	15
Fullerton	10	6	2	2	30	16	14

It was clear to those who were studying it carefully around the noticeboard that Tanby needed only to draw against them to clinch the Championship.

'That makes them the favourites,' confirmed Andrew. 'We've got to beat them to win it.'

'So what? It won't make it any easier for them,' answered Scott. 'You can't go out to play for a draw, it's too risky. They'll have to try to win.'

'And that'll give us more of a chance,' joined in Jeff positively. 'What a cracker it'll be!'

'There's a medal for the champions,' said Paul, back at school again and regretting missing the big win. 'It'd be great to have one of those to keep.'

'Well there's only Tanby to stop us, that's all,' joked Graham. 'But at least we should have Alan and Gary this time to help us.'

In the meantime, though, there was

plenty of work to undertake in the class-room, and the children had to buckle down and try to concentrate on that. It was a very busy time of year, especially for the footballers, who were practising hard outside the classroom on the playing fields besides rustling up plenty of support for the big match the following week.

Tanby on the other hand were occupied with another key game on this Saturday, and Mr Kenning offered to take four boys in his car to watch their Cup Final against Fairway. Jeff, Scott, Graham and Dale didn't have to be asked twice!

'Great!' responded Dale. 'We can try to spot all their weaknesses!'

Mr Kenning laughed. 'Well, perhaps, but at least we can all enjoy the game.'

It was indeed an excellent match, but as much as the boys enjoyed it, they couldn't help wishing it might have been them playing instead.

164

'I reckon we could have beaten Fairway this time,' said Graham.

'So do I, Tanby are winning easily – they're pretty good, aren't they?' replied Jeff, wondering about their own chances against them next week.

Tanby proved too good indeed on the day for Fairway. From being level at half-time Tanby powered on to dominate the Final and take the Cup 3-1.

As Jeff watched the captain Simon Walsh receive the trophy and lift it happily above his head to the cheers of the spectators, he

wished with all his heart he could swap places with him. It made him all the more determined that his own turn would come next Saturday. It would be a lifelong dream come true, and any thought now of possible defeat never entered his head.

As they returned home they were all strangely quiet. Mr Kenning wondered whether a few butterflies were already beginning to flutter about in their stomachs. He would have to ensure they were fully occupied in class next week to take their minds off the game a little!

He tried to perk them up now with the mention of their suspect left back. 'He didn't play very well again today, I thought,' he said. 'Robert Jackson did well against him last time, and David should do even better.'

Jeff nodded in agreement. 'We'll tell Dave – he can look forward to giving him the run-around.'

After dropping the boys off near the village green, Mr Kenning couldn't help but smile as he drove slowly past one of the shops and glanced at the window. It was owned by the Robinsons and he had been attracted by a huge poster in the middle of it, with the brothers' colourful artwork all over it.

'DON'T MISS THE GREAT MATCH!' it read over a large picture of a trophy and goalposts. 'SANDFORD v TANBY – THE LEEGUE CHAMPIONSHIP DECIDER. KO 10 O'CLOCK!

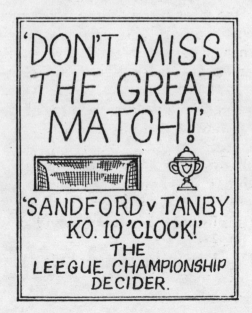

'I shall have to teach them how to spell *League* properly,' chuckled Mr Kenning. 'But at least the facts are right. One week to go and then it will all be settled, one way or the other. Quite a game with which to end the season,' he mused.

But even he didn't realize just what a dramatic match lay ahead.

11 The Championship Decider

Preparation for the final big match was as usual – the boys continuing to practise hard at the basic skills of the game, trying to improve their passing and control. Monday's session finished with a seven-a-side game, the highlight of which was a cracking goal from Alan on the volley.

'Great!' shouted Scott. 'We'll have one of those on Saturday too.'

Tackling was always just as keen as if they were in a real match, and any accidental knocks taken were accepted in good spirit. Everyone was hoping to be in the team, and Mr Kenning was delighted to see that Gary was fully established as a vital member of the squad and included as a friend by them all. They now knew what he was capable of.

The teacher thought long and hard about team selection, but eventually stuck to the eleven that had played so well together recently, which meant naming Gary, reluctantly, with Ian, as substitute. The talented striker would be their 'secret weapon' on the touchline, and even just seeing him there ready to come on might well be enough to worry the Tanby lads!

News arrived that Fairway had only drawn their last game so, whatever the result, the top two League places would be decided by Saturday's clash. The trophy, winners' medals and runners-up certificates could now be presented straight after the match to make it a memorable occasion.

So the scene was set, and the Saturday morning seemed perfect as Mr Kenning arrived early on a pleasantly warm March day to fix up the nets and prepare the refreshments.

But matters soon took a turn for the worse. As the boys and some spectators began to arrive and anticipation built up, Mr Fisher brought in Andrew, who was limping slightly.

'He fell down some steps at home last night, I'm afraid,' the father said apologetically. 'It's up to you whether you think he's fit to play or not.'

The teacher's heart sank. He sighed and looked at Andrew who was most upset. 'What a time to choose to trip over,' he said, trying to raise a smile. 'How does it feel?'

'My ankle hurts a bit, but I can run on it OK,' Andrew answered. 'I've got a bandage on, supporting it.'

'Let's try you out on the playground. Come on.'

The other boys followed, downcast at possibly losing the solid, strong tackles of Andrew at the back. They watched him running and turning and kicking a ball,

and he was trying so hard to hide any discomfort he may have felt that Mr Kenning had to be impressed by his determination to play.

'All right, Andrew, I want you to play . . .' he began as the boy's face instantly lit up. '*But,* the moment I think you're in some pain or not playing as well as you normally do we'll have you off. Is that clear? We don't want to make the injury any worse.'

Andrew nodded with relief, and began to change straightaway before Mr Kenning could change his mind.

It was a risk, but Andrew deserved the chance to start the game at least. Ian was there as stand-by luckily too. At that moment Tanby arrived with plenty of support, and so did Mr Robson, the League organizer, who was acting as the neutral referee.

There was a large gathering of people by the time the two teams reached the pitch, having made a detour on the way to admire the trophy glittering in the sunshine.

'This is it. Good luck to you all, and keep playing football as well as you know how,' encouraged Mr Kenning after the pre-match warm up. 'Go out and enjoy it. Let's hope it's our day today.'

'It will be,' stated Jeff, simply. 'We'll do it. C'mon, let's get at them!'

With his favourite rallying cry they were off, and the game was quickly under way with a flurry of activity in front of both goals. First Tanby had a shot deflected wide by Andrew, who lunged across to get a foot to a skidding ball. It was an important interception as Ricky hadn't had it covered properly, but unfortunately Andrew was limping again after he stood up.

The corner was cleared and Sandford broke crisply away, Scott finding Dale who switched it back to Graham. He made good

ground before releasing the ball to Alan, and as the blond striker sidestepped one tackle he hit the ball on the half-volley. It looked a goal all the way until Kevin Baker, their athletic keeper, dived to his left and clung on to it superbly.

David immediately troubled the left back, nipping round him to send a long, dipping shot just over the bar, and soon afterwards crossing for Alan to turn the ball only centimetres wide of a post.

But then Tanby went ahead. On the break Simon Walsh, the skipper, slid the ball expertly inside Jimmy for their winger to run on to and shoot powerfully past Ricky. The visitors whooped their delight, but Jeff rallied his team straightaway. 'C'mon, never mind. Let's go and get the equalizer. Keep tighter on him, Jimmy.'

But a goal would not come for them, and in fact, Ricky became the busier of the two goalkeepers.

174

Then Sandford received a disappointing setback. After Ricky made a tremendous save from a point-blank range shot, Andrew had to come to the rescue for a second time by clearing the loose ball off the line. But the corner was a bad one, going straight behind for a goal kick. As always, Sandford marked tightly goal-side in case the kick should be mis-hit, and this time Ricky did slip as he connected.

Normally Andrew would have reached the ball first and dealt with the danger, but now he seemed a little slow to react and as the forward moved on to it Andrew's ankle gave way as he turned. His opponent made no mistake with such a gift chance and the home supporters were in despair, their side 0-2 down and Andrew lying painfully on the ground, near to tears.

'I hurt it again when I cleared the ball,' he moaned as Mr Kenning inspected his ankle. 'I'm sorry. I was looking at my

foot when the kick was taken.'

'All right, no good worrying now,' consoled the teacher, knowing the lad had done his best. 'It wasn't your fault, but you'd better come off to rest it.'

He limped off to sit gloomily next to his father, and Ian – so useful a member of the squad – slotted easily into his place at the back. But the prospects now looked bleak, especially when it was almost three as the ball hit a post in a goalmouth scramble. Tanby were rampant.

'That's the way,' bellowed Mr Brown, their teacher. 'Let's have another – you've got them reeling!'

Certainly for a while Sandford seemed disorganized but they kept their heads and gradually began to settle down once more, trying all the time to play skilful football. They appeared to have earned their reward when Alan netted from Dale's cross but the referee had blown for offside, cutting their celebrations short.

Gary was kicking idly at the ground on the touchline, not really concentrating on the game. The teacher was tempted to use him already but it was still too early. He was glad he resisted it because a few minutes before half-time they had the ball in the net again, and this time it counted.

John and Jeff worked the ball out to David, who feinted to go inside the full back but then suddenly cut outside and was away. With everyone expecting a cross, they were caught unawares as the ball curled over their heads and sailed into

the far top corner of the goal. It was a remarkable effort which David convincingly claimed was intended, and not just a lucky centre as his team-mates joked at half-time.

Tanby remained confident of doing the Double despite that goal, still riding the crest of a wave after their Cup Final victory, but it had put fresh heart into Sandford to discover that Baker was not unbeatable!

'Have more shots,' encouraged Mr Kenning. 'He won't save them all. Keep going, well done so far.'

Nobody had criticized Andrew at all, and he was more cheerful now standing next to Gary who had also perked up considerably with the promise that he would be on soon.

Tanby began well again, attacking strongly down the right, but first Paul and then Ian broke up useful moves with well-timed tackles. Despite his hat-trick in the previous game Dale was finding little scope against a rugged right back and wasn't being given much opportunity to shine. Sandford's attack was slowly being squeezed out of the match, and even Alan failed to make his usual impact.

Jeff tried hard to encourage them but only David looked likely to break the stranglehold. It was just as well that Scott was playing an inspired game in defence, always in the thick of the action and lifting the performance of those around him too.

But something extra was badly needed in attack, and Mr Kenning decided that Dale would have to come off to make room for Gary. Dale was disappointed, but wished Gary luck as they passed while the spectators gave him a special round of applause.

Gary hadn't needed any instructions about where or how to play. He would play the only way he knew, the Gary

Clarke way, and the teacher was fervently hoping that he would click into top gear today. 'Go out and show them what you can do,' was all he said.

Gary grinned, and behind that burned the determination to do just that. This was his great chance to earn some glory!

Although Tanby were dismayed to see Gary's entry, he was heavily tackled and easily robbed the first time he touched the ball, and with relief they thought he wasn't going to be such a problem after all.

But gradually the spectators sensed a shift in the delicate balance of the game as Sandford began to put more fluent moves together and increase in confidence. And it was that painful tackle that motivated Gary into real action. He received the ball next time in space in the centre circle, and instead of looking for someone to pass to as expected, he decided to test them out and headed straight for goal. Taken by surprise, their defenders back-pedalled rapidly and finally managed to crowd him out. But that piece of opportunism was enough to inspire his own team-mates and to instil the first seeds of doubt into the minds of their opponents.

Sandford applied more and more pressure and suddenly the sides were level. Jeff had a shot charged down but Gary's speed off the mark enabled him to reach the loose ball first and stab it square into Graham's path. This was Sandford's leading goal-scorer's favourite position, closing in mercilessly with the ball teed up just inside the area. He struck it fiercely and his ninth League goal flashed into the net.

As Graham was swamped beneath his jubilant pals some of their friends in the crowd took up the rhythmic chant of 'Sandford! Sandford! Sandford!'

Two-all, but Jeff was quick to remind

everyone that a point was still enough to make Tanby the Champions. 'C'mon, a draw's no good to us, we've got to win. We want another goal.'

There were only a dozen minutes left to go and Tanby's Mr Brown was shouting instructions to his team to hold out.

In fact Tanby did more than just hold out. They attacked back, gained a corner, and from this a powerful drive beat Ricky, and Paul instinctively dived across behind him to try and stop it. Unfortunately, however, he accidentally kept it out with his hand!

He lay on the line face down, listening sorrowfully to the cries of *'Penalty!'* all around him. The referee had no choice but to award one.

Ian consoled Paul with a pat on the back. 'Can't be helped, you didn't mean to. Great save, though, you'll have to play in goal next year!'

The players spread out along the penalty area line as Simon Walsh prepared to take the kick and Ricky crouched tensely, ready to spring. 'This is like the Sevens final all over again!' he thought. 'But this time the goal is bigger!'

As the spectators grew hushed, Ricky decided to dive to his left where he had saved Simon's penalty that day and hope for a repeat. The Tanby captain ran up and struck it cleanly. The gamble was correct. Ricky got a hand to the ball and turned it on to the post, but as a mixture of cheers and groans went up from the crowd, the penalty-taker recovered quickly. Before Ricky could scramble to his feet, Simon had pounced upon the rebound and lashed it into the net with great relish. The applause was equally generous for both boys.

'Hard luck, pal,' said Jeff as he helped Ricky up again. 'Great effort at first.' They tried to smile but they knew they were

really up against it now.

'It looks like Tanby's game,' remarked Jeff's father.

'Maybe, but we're not down yet,' replied Mr Kenning. 'Not if I know your Jeff and the rest of the lads.'

Shrugging off this setback Sandford renewed their attacks. Perhaps Tanby began to think it was all settled now that they were ahead again because for the first time in the match their play became sloppy and casual.

'Concentrate!' warned Mr Brown. 'Be careful!'

But his words were too late. They had lost their edge and it allowed Gary to seize his opportunity. He hit a scything pass out to David who quickly returned a low fast centre. It was too speedy, though, for anyone to make contact and seemed about to fly out of danger when suddenly Gary appeared from nowhere to smack the ball on the volley with his right foot, falling over as he connected.

He caught it with perfect timing and stunning power in the middle of his boot and the ball was bouncing back out of the net before Kevin Baker had even moved. The supporters too were taken by surprise at first, then they let out a tremendous cheer and Gary was hauled off the floor by his excited teammates.

'What a goal! What a goal!' yelled Jeff. 'A Gary Clarke special right on cue.'

Mr Kenning was as thrilled as the rest with that moment of brilliance out of the blue. Three goals each with five minutes remaining – the League title was back in the balance . . .

The goal shook Tanby back to their senses and they tightened up again to try and survive to the end. Both teams were very tired now.

Jimmy won a tackle on the right, having

shut his winger out of the game since that first goal, and played the ball up to John, who then helped it on to Alan. Seeing the keeper off his line he lobbed it expertly towards goal. But to Sandford's horror and dismay the ball clipped the top of the crossbar and passed over. Sandford now were completely dominant, and Tanby were happy to kick the ball away anywhere.

They were so near to winning the Championship, and yet perhaps so far; and so it proved. Gary managed to win the ball by tackling back in midfield – it was a rare event for Gary to do such work – and switched it left into Graham's path as he moved menacingly into the opponents' half. Graham drew three players towards him, including the right full back, and then suddenly swung the ball out to the left wing.

'Oh no!' thought Mr Kenning. 'He's forgotten Dale's not there any more.' And then his mouth dropped open in surprise

186

.as he saw Jeff Thompson swoop on to it and speed away down the flank.

'What on earth is he doing out there?' he said aloud in amazement. 'Where did he come from?'

Jeff himself couldn't really have explained. He'd simply drifted out wide as Graham cut inside. Now he unexpectedly found himself with a clear path to goal, the defence wrong-footed by Graham's clever change of direction.

As the centre-half started to move desperately across, and the excellent keeper came out to narrow the angle even more than it already was, Jeff realized he had no choice. Although he was on his weaker left foot, he had to shoot immediately or the chance would be smothered and lost for ever.

He hit the ball in full stride, hopefully wide of the goalkeeper. Jeff saw him touch it before tumbling over, but managed to

recover in time to see the ball strike the inside of the far post high up and deflect inwards to nestle comfortably in the bottom corner of the Tanby net.

Jeff, still on his knees, threw his hands into the air in triumph, and then found himself lifted up and almost carried back to the halfway line by the rest of his delirious team, including Ricky who had raced out to add his excitement to the group.

The poor Tanby players could hardly believe what had happened as they realized that all was lost. Their heads went down and Alan almost made it five when his shot, the last of the game, slithered only just wide.

The final whistle sounded to give Sandford a remarkable 4-3 victory in the finest game seen in the area for many years, and both teams were loudly applauded all the way off the field. Among all the celebrations and consolations, the two captains found themselves side by side and they shook hands. Simon Walsh managed a smile. 'Great goal, Jeff, at the end.'

'Well, you've got the Cup; now we've won the League. I reckon that makes us about even,' replied Jeff happily.

As Jeff was asked to step forward to

receive the trophy a few minutes later he did so in a dream, the cheering ringing in his head. He proudly held the prize up high in both hands and basked in the glorious moment of success. Nothing could compare with such a feeling and the grin on his face stretched almost from ear to ear!

It was time then for all of them to go up in turn to collect their individual medals and certificates as souvenirs of a great day and a memorable season, and just before they gathered together for a few photographs Jeff yelled out, 'Three cheers for Mr Kenning!' The whole Sandford team responded heartily in front of their laughing teacher.

The celebrations continued back in the changing room where both teams were joining in the noisy chanting of *'We are the Champions!'* and *'We've won the Cup!'*, all friends together now that the rivalry on the field was over.

At the Monday morning assembly the Championship trophy stood on the Hall table for everyone to see as the school applauded the squad of footballers for their successful season. From the side of the room Mr Kenning looked with satisfaction at each of the happy, proud faces of the boys as they stood up in their places to receive the well-deserved praise.

'How things have changed since that first September morning,' reflected the teacher. 'It all seems so very long ago – so much has happened since then.'

He switched his gaze from one to another, and finally from the amazing captain Jeff to the equally astonishing wonder-boy Gary! How much the players had grown up and improved in so many ways.

Some of them would soon leave this school for their next, but others would return to be the main strength in a new group of lads to try all over again the following season. In the meantime of course there was the approaching summer term to enjoy, with the different pleasures and excitements of cricket and athletics.

Mr Kenning sat back contentedly in his seat. He was looking forward to all that, but this present soccer season was not over yet.

Just ahead of them in the Easter holidays lay another great adventure. The footballers of Sandford Primary School were about to go on tour!

THE END

Appendix

Results and Goal Scorers
League Matches

Sandford 2 – 2 Fairway
Parthorpe 0 – 6 Sandford
Sandford 5 – 1 Ullesby
Fullerton 4 – 2 Sandford
Sandford 2 – 0 The Park
St John's 2 – 5 Sandford
Sandford 4 – 0 Kelworth
Scotney 1 – 4 Sandford
Sandford 1 – 1 Little Beaton
Gainsville 1 – 7 Sandford
Sandford 4 – 3 Tanby

	P	W	D	L	F	A	Pts
Sandford	11	8	2	1	42	15	18

League Scorers

Graham Ford 9, Dale Gregson 7, David Woodward 7, Jeff Thompson 5, Alan Clayton 4, John Robinson 4, Gary Clarke 3, Paul Curtis 1, Dean Walters 1, +1 own goal.

Frisborough Cup

1st Round : Kelworth 1 – 3 Sandford
2nd Round : Fullerton 1 – 2 Sandford
Semi-Final : Sandford 1 – 2 Tanby

Cup Scorers

Dale Gregson 2, Graham Ford 1, David Woodward 1, Gary Clarke 1, Scott Peters 1.